Crime of Passion 2

Lock Down Publications and Ca$h
Presents

Crime of Passion 2

A Novel by *Mimi*

Crime of Passion 2

Lock Down Publications

P.O. Box 870494
Mesquite, Tx 75187

Visit our website @
www.lockdownpublications.com

Copyright 2019 by Crime of Passion 2

All rights reserved. No part of this book may be reproduced in any form or by electronic or mechanical means, including information storage and retrieval systems without permission in writing from the publisher, except by a reviewer who may quote brief passages in review.
First Edition February 2019
Printed in the United States of America

This is a work of fiction. Names, characters, places, and incidents either are products of the author's imagination or are used fictitiously. Any similarity to actual events or locales or persons, living or dead, is entirely coincidental.

Lock Down Publications
Like our page on Facebook: Lock Down Publications @
www.facebook.com/lockdownpublications.ldp
Cover design and layout by: **Dynasty Cover Me**
Book interior design by: **Shawn Walker**
Edited by: **Jill Alicea**

3

Mimi

Stay Connected with Us!

Text **LOCKDOWN** to 22828 to stay up-to-date with
new releases, sneak peaks, contests and more…
Thank you.

Warning This material may cause triggers as it has to deal with domestic violence.

~Dedication~

Writing this book took me on a journey. Not many people know that I was in a domestic violence relationship, and while none of what is in this book is what I went through, I know that it may be true for most. I want to dedicate this book to all the domestic violence survivors and to the women who may still be going through it. Most times we feel like there is no way to leave, but I'm telling you that YOU can and that it is OKAY to LEAVE! You are not alone!

To my readers, thank you for giving me the opportunity to allow me to deliver you some heat! I work extremely hard and work my fingers to the bone to give you nothing but the best.

To my LDP fam, thank y'all for always holding it down and supporting me from the gate! It's an LDP thang, baby, and I look forward to growing with all y'all! XoXo

If you or anyone that you know is being subjected to abuse, speak up and speak out by calling the Domestic Violence Hotline at 1-800-799-7233 (SAFE)

You are a survivor!

Mimi

Chapter One

Now they say congratulations
Worked so hard, forgot how to vacation
They ain't never had the dedication
People hatin', say we changed and look, we made it

Four years, multiple loans, debt, and countless nights of no sleep finally paid off. I sat in the audience with my fellow graduates and looked around and smiled at everyone in their black cap and gowns. We were all graduating with Bachelor's degrees and were ready to take the world by storm. My eyes landed on my best friend Keana. She was a few rows behind me and she looked nervous. I shook my head with a smirk on my face and continued to listen to our dean, Miles Clark, give the same speech he made every year. I just wanted to get across the stage.

Forty-five minutes later and they were finally wrapping up the speeches and getting ready to call the graduates. My palms grew sweaty and I looked out into the sea of faces. I couldn't spot my mother, who was my only supporter besides Keana and her family. As my mind wandered to how much support I got from the little bit of people I had, it made my eyes mist over.

"Mah'lani Carter!" the dean yelled my name.

Not only did my mother and Keana's family roar in excitement, but every one of my peers stood up, clapping and yelling. A smile formed on my face as I walked across the stage to receive my degree. The tears wouldn't stay contained as I made it back to my seat. Using the tips of my fingers, I patted my eyes so as not to smudge my makeup.

Several minutes later, the dean yelled Keana's name. And just like she did for me, I stood up and acted like a plumb fool.

Of course, everyone joined in as we watched Keana do a praise dance across the stage. We had worked so hard for this moment, so I completely understood why she caught the Holy Ghost.

In less than fifteen minutes, we were placing our tassels onto the left side of our hats and were leaving. I met up with Keana so that we could meet our families together.

"Bitch, we made it!" Keana yelled as she ran and jumped into my arms, almost knocking me over.

"Girl, I should beat your ass. I almost fell." I giggled. I unzipped my gown, took it off, and draped it over my arm.

"Damn, look at all that ass!" she yelled and smacked my ass.

Bending at the waist, I wiggled my ass. Bursting into giggles, we made our way to go find our peoples. They were standing in a circle holding balloons and flowers, chatting away and waiting for us. My mother was the first to see us and she screamed. She ran into my arms and hugged me tight.

For as long as I could remember, it had always been me and Mama. She never spoke about my father and I never asked about him. She volunteered to tell me that he decided that her choosing to have me was such a curse that he left even before I was born.

My mama worked her fingers to the bone to make sure that I had everything. I never had to ask for nothing because she bought it before I could even try to fix my mouth to ask for it. If we ever went through a struggle, I never saw it due to the fact my mama never showed it. Food was always on the table, and we always had a roof over our heads and clothes on our backs. My mama was everything that I hoped to become as an adult. She was my backbone.

From the middle of elementary school up until I got into high school, I got bullied horribly. It was never about my clothes, my hair, or my hygiene. It was because my whole life, I always had extra meat on my bones. I came home crying one day and my mama wanted to know why. I was nine and I explained that we had a new student and he had targeted me. That day she grilled me like never before. She told me that I was beautiful in the skin that I was in. Whether I was skinny, big, tall, short, dark, or light, I was beautiful no matter what. She told me that if I believed that, can't nobody tell me nothing. Even though I was bullied well into my high school years, I owned it. Granted, most times it ended in me being suspended for fighting, but at the end of it all, I kept my confidence and wore it well.

Now at twenty-six, I weighed in at two hundred and forty-seven pounds and I stood at 5'8" inches tall. All my weight resided in my hips, thighs, and ass because my stomach was nice and flat. Naturally my hair was long, past my shoulders, but I kept it in a twenty-six-inch Brazilian weave. My skin was the color of honey and my eyes were the lightest shade of brown. I was far from an ugly duckling and I knew for sure that I was some dude's cup of tea. My confidence was through the roof and nobody could tell me otherwise.

"I am so proud of you two," Keana's mom, Mama Anita, spoke.

"Thank you," both Keana and I answered.

Keana was like my sister, since I was an only child. She had younger siblings and eventually they became like mine too. Keana's dad, Poppa Nate, was my father figure and I couldn't be any happier than what I had been since meeting them.

"We are going to go to Bomber's and get some food. Afterwards, you ladies are free to do whatever it is your heart desires," my mama mentioned.

"Good, 'cause I could eat," Rayshawn, Keana's brother said.

With a smile on all our faces, we walked out of the theater where our graduation was being held. To Bomber's we went.

Chapter Two

Look, I might just chill in some Bape
I might just chill with your boo
I might just feel on your babe
My pussy feel like a lake

As Keana and I got ready to leave to go hit up Andy's in Albany, we got hyped and danced around listening to Cardi B's "Bodak Yellow". We had a reason to celebrate, and that's just what we planned to do. We were at my house sipping on Jose Cuervo and orange juice. Luckily there was Uber and Lyft because neither of us would be chauffeur for the night.

I was at the mirror flat-ironing my hair and Keana was still deciding what to wear. We had an hour to leave and at the rate she was going, we wouldn't be leaving until midnight. The music paused, indicating that I had a call coming through. I reached for my phone and saw that it was Mark calling.

Mark was my "something to do" when I was bored. He'd never gotten the nookie, but the way he blew me up on a constant basis, you would think he had. Mark was only able to smell the punany and on some occasions, taste it. I was a proud virgin. It wasn't like I was saving myself for marriage or anything, but I did want to lose my virginity to someone who I felt was special let's not forget, someone who I considered myself to be in love with.

"Who's that?" Keana asked, catching the aggravated look I had on my face.

"Mark's irritating ass," I answered as I placed my phone on the dresser. The music resumed and so did we.

Keana, who was a shade lighter than I and had flawless skin, was dressed in black with red flowers, slightly baggy joggers, a white crop top, and six-inch open toe stiletto's that strapped at the ankle. Her hair was up in a top knot and she had choppy bangs. She wore gold accessories to complement her outfit.

I was dressed in light-colored jean shorts that had a little distress to them and a gold halter top that had tassels hanging from it. I placed my feet in a comfortable pair of black and gold Steve Madden wedges. After I placed in my diamond stud earrings, we grabbed our clutches and left to go wait for our Uber outside. My mother, who had stayed over at Keana's house, was pulling into the driveway while we were waiting. She jumped out and began to take pictures of us.

"Okay, I see y'all," she kept saying as she kept snapping, causing Keana and I to bust out in a fit of giggles as we began to pose.

"Alright, Mama. Our Uber is here. We got to go. Don't wait up," I said, placing a kiss on her cheek.

"Oh, please, child. I got me a little piece of chocolate coming on through."

I paused in my footsteps and turned around. I placed my hand on my hip and said, "Excuse me. Since when did you decide to have little pieces of anything coming this way?"

My mama matched my stance and said, "I'm grown and do what I want."

"Lani, come on! Leave your mama alone!" Keana yelled from the back of the Uber.

"We gonna talk about this in the morning!" I yelled, getting inside of the car. My mother laughed and walked inside of the house.

For the longest, I had never seen my mother with a guy. She was a woman and had needs, but I had never seen her with anyone. Not even in my teen years did I wake up to some strange man in the house. After some time, I even considered that maybe my mother to like to bump coochies. She always had her girlfriends over on the weekends, but never no dudes. Eventually, I just stopped paying attention to what she was doing and focused on making her proud.

Keana made jokes all the way to Andy's and I never wanted to punch her in her throat so bad.

"Alright now, keep hee-heeing, and I hope Mama Alicia and Pop Nate pop out another baby on your ass," I spoke as I climbed out of the Uber.

"Bitch, I think the fuck not. They gonna fuck around and break a hip to create one."

"You think that they don't be getting they shit off like your freak nasty ass?"

"Oh my God, Mah'lani! Never mind. Let's just drop it."

Side-eyeing Keana, I looked at her and said, "Oh, so now that I'm talking about your parents getting they rocks off, you want to change the subject. Alright, cool. We can do that too. Stay off my mama."

"Tell that chocolate nigga that your mama got coming to stay off of her," Keana whispered, thinking that I didn't hear her.

"Bitch, you lucky you my sister 'cause you were about to get popped right in the mouth like you were my child," I responded with my hand up like I was about to pop her.

Seconds later, we busted out laughing and walked inside of Andy's. This wasn't our first time out to Andy's, and it was one of our favorite spots. It was a small bar and not too many people frequented it, so it was perfect for us. The bar sat in the middle of the floor with tables and stools against the walls. In the front by the window was a dartboard, and TV's adorned the perimeter of the walls and over the bar. Keana and I made our way over and took a seat.

"What can I get you ladies?" the bartender yelled over the bass of Yo Gotti's "Rake It Up".

"We'll both have rum and Coke, little ice, and two double shots of Hennessy," Keana ordered for the both of us.

"Coming right up."

At most, there were ten people just vibing out and this was why we chose to come to this bar. I signaled for the bartender to come back and placed an order for hot wings. After grabbing our drinks, we went to the music box and selected twelve songs that we wanted to listen to before anyone had the chance to put something on that we didn't want to hear.

Slowly, Andy's began to get crowded, which was unusual, but by this time, it was midnight, and Keana and I were feeling nice. Somebody had made a mistake and put on "Back That Ass Up" by Juvenile. Keana and I made complete fools out of ourselves as we hollered and began to throw our asses in a circle. Most of the girls that joined us were cutting up too. The fellas just watched with smirks on their faces. I'm a thick chick but not sloppy, and my ass was moving something crazy. Keana stopped dancing just to hype me up and as usual, the chicks that were dancing started shading because they weren't getting attention.

"Aye! Yes, best friend! Fuck it up!" Keana yelled, clapping her hands as I planted my feet, placed my hands behind my head, interlocked my fingers, and wound my hips fast.

Everyone's attention immediately went to me. Some girl with a long, nappy synthetic ponytail and bang that wasn't properly installed to where you could see her tracks was coming my way. Her toes were hanging over her shoes and I knew by now she must have rubbed the skin off her toes. I still heard Keana hyping me up and as I turned to slap fives with her, I got pushed. Not a little nudge; I'm talking about pushed to where I fell to one knee and had to save face and pop back up, that kind of push. The girl who pushed me had scurried to a corner with a bunch of her lame-ass friends. I heard Keana asking if I was okay but at that moment, I couldn't bother to answer. All I saw was that group of girls standing in the corner, pointing and laughing. Keana was holding onto my arm. Yanking loose from her grip, I began to make my way to those hood rats.

"So, you think that shit was funny?" I asked upon reaching them. I knew this one chick was the ringleader by how she was in front of the group. She stepped closer to me with her arms folded across her chest.

"Lani, let's just go somewhere else. We out here trying to celebrate and there ain't no need for these bitches to ruin that," Keana expressed.

She was right. In just a few days, I was going to be starting my job as a social worker at the Schenectady County Department of Social Services. I just knew this hoe would be the cause of me catching a case. I looked at Keana and she nodded to me to let me know that it was okay to take this loss. With everything in me, I turned around and began to walk away, until this hoe decided to grow some balls.

"Your fat ass shouldn't have been in my way in the first place." She laughed, causing her friends to join in.

It wasn't about her calling me fat. I couldn't care less about that. What tripped me out was the fact that she felt the need to say it as I was walking away.

Pausing in my footsteps, I turned around and Keana let me go. She knew that I hated when people would try to say something to your back rather than to your face. I stepped so close to her that if I came in any closer, we'd practically be kissing.

"What did you say?" I asked. By this time, the bar was quiet, and all the attention was on this troll and me.

"You heard exactly what I said, obviously, or you wouldn't be all in my face right now."

Before I could get anything out of my mouth, this fine dude came and stood between us. He was so much taller than me that I had to strain my neck just to look up into his face. Give or take he was at least 6'7" tall and looked to be almost three hundred pounds of muscle. He was brown-skinned with medium light brown eyes and a bushy beard that was lined to precision. On his head he was rocking a black dad hat that sat covering almost half of his face. He was rocking a white tee and faded blue jeans with crisp all-white Nike Huarache's.

"Y'all shouldn't be in here getting ready to brawl." He spoke with the deepest voice I had ever heard.

Instantly, I felt a puddle beginning to form between my legs. My mouth was open, and I didn't realize it until Keana leaned in and told me so.

"This fat bitch shouldn't have been in my way," Nappy Weave stated, bringing my attention back to what was going on.

"Listen here, little girl. I'm fat, yes, anybody can see that. But what you not gonna do is keep adding bitch to the end of that! I suggest you and your friends go on 'bout y'all business, 'cause I'm telling y'all right now, y'all don't want this work."

Tall, fine, sexy dude looked down at me and said, "Shorty, you look like you have a more sensible head on your shoulders. Just walk away from this one."

"Nah! She wanted to wait until I walked away to say something. She so bad though, right!"

"If you walk away, then I will take care of your tab for the night."

He immediately had my attention and I stared at him. I nodded and began to turn away.

This bitch wouldn't let me be great. She pulled me by my hair, causing Keana to reach over me and clock that heifer upside her head. Two more husky men came up to us and pulled

Keana and the girl apart while tall and fine was holding me back from ripping this bitch to shreds.

"Bitch, you got this one! But let me catch you in these streets, it's on sight! And while you at it, fix that tragedy on top of your head! Scarecrow looking-ass bitch!" I yelled as Tall and Fine dragged me out of the bar. Soon Keana followed, trying to fight the nigga that was bringing her out.

"Nigga, get your hands off me! Our shit is still in there!" she yelled.

"Randy, can you go back in there and get these ladies their things and settle their tab?" Tall and Fine spoke to the guy handling Keana.

"Why do we have to leave when those bitches were the ones who started it?" Keana asked. She was fired up and wanted answers. She was worse than me when angry. By this time, I had calmed down and was leaning against a car that sat out front.

"Keana, let's just call it a night. We gonna see that bitch again soon enough. Let's just drop this, get an Uber, and go and get something to eat." My feet were hurting and all I wanted was food and my bed.

"Fine. But all of my shit better be where it's supposed to be, or this whole fucking block is gonna go up in flames."

Tall and Fine turned to me and flashed a smile with perfect white teeth. *He must have had braces when he was younger. Or his parents had some really nice teeth,* I thought to myself.

He spoke in a deep, sensual voice. "Why take an Uber when Randy and I can accompany you ladies and we could be your ride?"

Turning up my lips, I spoke. "We don't know you."

"That's the whole point of me extending that request to you. You a feisty little thing and I would love to get to know you better."

Mimi

Randy caught our attention when he came out with our things. Both Keana and I checked to see if anything was missing from our clutches and luckily for everybody that's on that block, we had everything. I turned my attention to Tall and Fine and said, "Let me speak with my homegirl about this."

He nodded his head, and I walked over to Keana and told her what Tall and Fine asked me. Keana was always down for a free meal, so of course she was down. I tossed the idea around in my head as I looked over at Randy and Tall and Fine as they were talking. He turned to me and displayed that perfect smile, slipping his bottom lip between his teeth. That's when my mind was made up. Keana and I made it back over to them and let them lead the way.

***

The sun was shining brightly on my face. The pounding in my head was a reminder as to why I should never overdo it when I drink. As I pulled the covers over my head, I felt a body lying next to me and I stiffened as I felt the weight of a leg over my shin. Peeking under the covers, I noticed that it was only Keana and relief washed over my body. Tossing the covers off me, I got up and headed to take care of my hygiene. Once I was done, I headed back into my room and put on some Nike sweatpants and a wife beater and headed to the kitchen.

My mama was sitting at the table, nursing a cup of coffee and reading a health magazine. She looked up at me with a smile on her face and I eyed her. I hadn't forgotten that she had some nigga up in here serving her up some dick. After making myself a cup of coffee, I joined her at the table.

"Good morning, Mah'lani. How was you and Keana's night?" she asked without looking up from the magazine.

18

"It was okay. We almost got into an all-out brawl at the bar, but it was stropped before I had to break a chick in half," I responded.

She looked up and asked, "What you mean? What the hell happened?"

"First, you let me know who the dude was that you had over last night. Out of all my years of living, I have never seen you with anybody. At one point, I even thought that maybe you had started to like women."

My mama looked at me with a straight face for several seconds and out of the blue, she let out a hearty laugh that caused her to hold her stomach. In between her laughter, she said, "Child, ain't nothing about me gonna ever allow another female between my legs or me in between another woman's legs. I'm strictly dickly. Mmm'kay!"

"So that still doesn't answer my questions, Mama." I eyed her over the rim of my mug as she dried tears from her eyes.

"Damn, Mah'lani, you nosy as hell. You don't see me sticking my nose into your affairs."

"That's because I don't have any affairs."

"From the way you and Keana was carrying on about some niggas named Dominic and Randy, it sounds like you will have some soon. And guess who gonna be all in the Kool-Aid, trying to find out the flavor?"

"Mama, that was so corny. Nobody says that, and please don't use that again. How and when did you hear Keana and me talking about Dominic and Randy?"

"Shit, y'all came in loud as hell at three this morning talking about those men. Wondering what they did for a living because they were pulling out plenty of knots."

"Oh my God!" I was embarrassed. The way my mama had said it made me seem like I was some chicken head. I couldn't help but wonder if I had done something to make myself look as such in front of Dominic. While I was trying to recall what happened when we arrived at Denny's on Wolf Road, Keana walked in, stretching, and made herself a cup of coffee.

"Mama Cheryl, what's wrong with this girl?" Keana asked.

"I told her that y'all came in talking about some dudes that took y'all to get something to eat."

"Oh, Randy and Dominic?"

"Yup. Those the ones."

"Keana, did I act a complete fool while at Denny's?" I asked. I couldn't remember shit after the incident at Andy's. Hell, I don't even remember how we got back in the house.

"No. You presented yourself as you would have if sober. You and that man kept giggling at each other. I thought we were back in high school. Randy and I made fun of y'all the whole time we were there and y'all didn't even know it."

"Oh, thank God! Back to you, Mama! Who was he?"

Exhaling, my mama got up from the table and washed her mug out. Placing it in the sink, she turned around to face us and lean against the counter. After she took her dramatic pause, she began to speak. "His name is Omar. I met him while I was out getting my car washed. We went out several times and I figured that being that you were finally going to be out of the house, I could invite him over for Netflix and chill."

"Eww," Keana and I said in unison.

"Y'all grown, we don't need to have the birds and the bees talk," Mama responded with her lips twisted up. She continued, "Y'all out here thotting and bopping, but I can't Netflix and chill?"

"Mama, you like a hundred years old. You need to sit down and chill before you break a hip," I said, causing myself and Keana to erupt in laughter.

My mama looked at me like she was ready to beat the shit out of me.

"Keep on. You ain't too old for me to whip your ass," she said as she walked out of the kitchen, causing us to laugh once again.

We cleaned the kitchen and headed on over to Keana's house to do our Netflix and chill while binging on junk food.

Mimi

Chapter Three

Flowers and gifts, restaurants,
I swear he buy me anything I want
That's why I'm so quick to
Put that music on for him, listen to it baby.

A long two weeks had passed since Keana and I had met Randy and Dominic. While Keana was trying to shake Randy, I hadn't even received a text from Dominic. I questioned if I even gave him my number or if I took his. Keana reassured me that he did take my number, so what was taking him so long to use it? After the first couple of days of not hearing from him, I told myself not to sweat it. If he was going to use my number, then he would when he wanted to.

As I sat at my desk looking over some cases, my supervisor walked into my office with a glass vase filled with lilies. For the past week, around the same time, I was receiving the same flowers. Mark was trying to get in contact with me since the flowers had started getting sent to my job. I wasn't taking his calls since I found out he was fucking around with another chick. Granted, he wasn't penetrating me, but we'd had plenty of conversations about me waiting to lose my virginity. I confronted Mark about what I had found out and he denied it. What he didn't know was that I had proof. The woman was bold enough to get my number from his phone and send me voice recordings of them talking before fucking and sending a picture of them cuddled up afterward. He'd been trying to contact me since and he'd been getting ignored. Sending the flowers - my favorite kind, at that - was wearing me down. In my mind, I thought I was beginning to miss him, and I thought maybe hearing him out wouldn't be so bad.

"Someone must be in the dog house," my supervisor, Clarissa, assumed.

She handed me the flowers and I couldn't help but think to myself, *That ain't none of your business.* After the first two days of working here, I knew she was messy. She knew that I knew how she got down due to me being in my office instead of meeting her and her crew at the water cooler, bumping their gums. I was there strictly to work and not talk about Wanda from across the building sucking on the janitor's dick while her lazy-ass husband stayed home and did nothing all day.

"Flowers doesn't necessarily mean someone messed up. He just adores me and wants to make sure to brighten my day with my favorite flowers," I lied. Like I said, it was none of her business.

"That is true. Listen, I came to not only bring you your flowers, but to invite you out to a girls' night out with myself and a few of the other girls here," she said.

"I actually have plans tonight with my best friend. I'm sorry I won't be able to make it."

"Well, if you change your mind, we will be having dinner at Bomber's and drinks at 151."

"You'll see me if I do," I responded with a smile plastered on my face. If she only knew that there was a better chance of hell freezing over than me going to hang out with the gossip girls. I was all the way good on that note. Clarissa walked out of my office and I got back to work.

Around two in the afternoon, I was getting ready to head to lunch when my phone chimed, indicating that I had a message. Instantly my eyes rolled because I just knew that it was Mark's ass. This time I was going to curse him out and put him in his place. To my surprise, it wasn't Mark. The number wasn't stored, so I didn't know who it was that sent it until I opened it up.

555-633-5714: Good afternoon, beautiful. First, I just want to apologize for waiting two weeks to get in touch with you. Since meeting you, you've been on my mind constantly. Yeah, I know that was corny, but it's the truth. I would love to take you out to dinner tonight, if you aren't busy.

~Dominic~

P.s I hope you enjoyed the flowers I've sent you this past week. ☺

The smile that appeared on my face could have been seen miles away. I sent him a quick thank you for the flowers and told him that I would like it if he took me out. After letting him know that I got off at six, I said bye and placed a call to Keana.

"Girl, what? You know damn well I can't be talking on this damn phone. You lucky I had to pee," Keana answered her phone.

"What kind of best friend are you, bitch?" I asked.

"Bitch, the only one to deal with your bullshit."

"Why did you give that man the address to where I work?"

Keana laughed and said, "Bitch, because he was busy and being that you haven't heard from him, I suggested that he send you flowers, you ungrateful hoe!"

"I'm gonna show you how ungrateful my ass is when I diss your ass to go on this date tonight!" I yelled through the phone as I exited the building.

"So he finally invited your funky stuck-up ass out? It's about time 'cause I'm tired of dealing with your ass."

"Fuck you, bitch. I guess I can let you go out tonight only because you are working both me and Mama Cheryl's nerves."

"You know what? I'm in a good mood and I will not allow your negativity to transmit over this way. Have a good day, whore," I said and hung up without letting her respond. I laughed all the way to my car.

My phone chimed, letting me know that I had a text message. After climbing into my car, I made my way to the nearest Taco Bell, grabbed a number ten, and made my way back to the office.

The gossip girls were huddled by the water cooler and ceased all talking when they saw me walking up. Sipping on my Baja Blast, I winked at them and walked into my office. Remembering I had a text message, I checked my phone, rolling my eyes after seeing that it had been Mark. Not even taking the energy to respond, I blocked him and enjoyed my Taco Bell.

***

Six o' clock came quicker than I expected, and I found myself packing my things and dancing my way out of the building. I stopped at the liquor store before I made it home. This body was going to soak in the tub for a half an hour before I got ready for my date with Dominic. My mama wasn't home when I had gotten there but when I entered my room, there was a garment bag on my bed and a black Gucci bag with shoes in it on the floor under the garment bag. On the dresser was a vase with lilies and a note and a card sat next to them. Opening the note first, I saw that it was from my mama. She said that the things that were in my room came for me today. She also thought it was cute to add that if a man was willing to buy a woman Gucci, he deserved some pussy. Rolling my eyes, I picked up the card and read that it was from Dominic. He told me to be ready at eight-thirty.

Kicking my shoes off, I took a couple of seconds to praise dance. After stripping out of my work clothes, I placed my bonnet on my head and went to shower. The bath soak was going to have to wait until the morning.

After my shower, I checked the time and it was nearing seven. I ran into the kitchen, grabbed a wine glass, and ran back into my room. I poured the wine in the glass and downed it. The second glass followed soon after to help my nerves. I opened the garment bag after I lotioned my body and admired the dress that was inside of the bag. It was white. My favorite color. The fabric felt so soft, I would have thought that Jesus made it himself. It clung to my body like a second skin. My back and shoulders were out, but there were sleeves. The dress stopped at my knees and hugged every curve. Waiting to put my shoes on, I applied a natural look to my face with a red lip. Next, I did some loose beach curls in my hair. I sat on my bed, took the shoebox out of the bag, and took the shoes out. They were cute, red peep toe platform stiletto's. A smile came across my face because although they were simple, they were super cute. Just like me. After placing the shoes on my feet, I stood up and looked at myself in the full-length mirror. I was impressed with the outcome. I took a few pictures, sent some to Keana, and then checked my messages. Dominic had sent a voice message letting me know that he would be through in ten minutes. I poured another glass of wine and cautiously sipped it, making sure not to spill any. Ten minutes later, Dominic texted me, letting me know he was outside. That was my cue to head on out.

There he was, standing against a white 2018 Lexus GS 460. He was dressed in navy blue Adidas track pants and matching jacket, a white tee resting under his jacket. He didn't have on a hat today and the lights from the light posts were beaming on his bald head. Today he had navy blue and white Air Max and once again, there were lilies. I walked towards him with a smile on my face and when I got close to him, he pulled me into a hug. *God, he smells good,* I thought.

"You look good as hell," Dominic said.

"Thank you. And you do too."

Dominic handed me the flowers and then opened the car door for me. "How was work?"

Rolling my eyes, I said, "Chicks at my job tried to pull me into their huddle party."

"Didn't you just start working there like two seconds ago?"

Giggling, I answered, "My point exactly. They tried to invite me out tonight."

"I hope that you told them that you were gonna be chilling with your possible new man."

"Well, at the time, I didn't know that Keana and you had this whole night planned out, so I used the best friend card."

"So, you figured that out?" Dominic chuckled.

"It wasn't hard. I figured it out once you texted me."

"I wanted to wait until we got to where we were going to apologize, but I think it's appropriate now. I didn't purposely not hit you up. Things have just been a little hectic. Like I've told you, I couldn't get you out of my mind, and that was the truth. Randy just so happened to invite Keana out to my bar and we happened to begin to talk about you. She suggested this date. I'm sorry for taking so long." Dominic glanced at me and smiled.

"I appreciate your apology, but I can assure you that it's not needed. I get that things come up. It's no big thing. Where are we going anyway?"

"Now that I can't tell you. From what Keana told me, you would like what I have planned."

"If not, you still have my interest. You won me over with the flowers, dress, and shoes." I laughed.

For the remainder of the ride, we made conversation about little things until we reached a restaurant that looked like it was closed. My eyebrows raised up and my mace was safe in my hand. The restaurant was called Gloria's and we were in Amsterdam.

"I see your whole demeanor changed. I can assure you that I'm not gonna hurt you. I own this restaurant," Dominic assured me. He reached for my hand and kissed the back of it. He climbed out of the truck and walked to my side and let me out.

I allowed my mace to drop to the bottom of my purse and stepped out of the truck. Dominic grabbed my hand and we walked to the door of the restaurant, where he used keys to open it. From the outside looking in, you would have thought there was no lighting, but at a table in the far-left corner, the light above the booth was dimly lit and candles adorned the table. After Dominic made sure that the doors were locked, we went further into the place.

The smells that were coming from the kitchen made my stomach turn with excitement. My mouth watered with anticipation. That's how bomb the restaurant smelled. Dominic led me in the direction of our table and pulled my chair out.

"Let me see how dinner is coming along. I will be back. Anything you would like to drink?" Dominic asked with sparkles dancing in his eyes.

"Any kind of red wine will be just fine." I smiled.

Without another word, he made his way into the kitchen. I was impressed. It had been a long while since I had been out on a date where a guy did all the things a gentleman is supposed to do. Not even Mark's simple ass did that. It was a refreshing feeling, to say the least. Going inside of my purse, I reached for my phone and out of habit, I texted Keana my location. Just to be on the safe side.

"I can't believe how amazing you look tonight. I thought you couldn't get any finer than the first night, but tonight you have honestly proved me wrong," he said, scaring the living daylights out of me.

"Ahh!" I screamed. Looking up at him, I continued, "I didn't even hear you come back. You scared the mess out of me."

"I didn't mean to. I apologize. Let me pour this wine before I end this date before it can truly begin."

"That won't happen. I'm enjoying your company."

"Mmm. Likewise. So, tell me some things about you?"

"Well, there's not really much to tell. I am an only child to my amazing mother. My father has never been around; I never met him. I graduated two weeks ago with a Bachelor's in social work. I'm a pretty simple girl and I just love to enjoy life," I explained.

"Where do you see yourself in five years?"

Damn, he's quick, I thought to myself. I sipped my wine and then cleared my throat, "Ultimately, my goal is to start a non-profit organization for girls of all ages to have a safe place to come to. I love kids, and if there is a way that I could help them, I would love to do that."

"What about boys? They go through things as well and there aren't many places that they can go to."

"I do understand that and over time, I would like to incorporate them into it, but my main focus is girls."

Dominic eyed me and sipped his wine. His gaze alone made me nervous and second guess my plan. Fuck that! I knew exactly what my plans and goals were, and can't nobody tell me otherwise.

Finally, he opened his mouth with a response. He said, "I like the fact that you are even considering including boys. Most of these knuckleheads are running around here with mothers who are on drugs and giving the police the 'police' to pull their weapons on them. We as a people – nah, scratch that, black people - we need to show the youth that there are people out here who care and want to see them become successful."

"Nowadays, it's way more important. Police killing black people faster than AIDS."

I was interrupted by the chef, who had come out to let us know that dinner was done. She gave us warm towels to clean our hands off and then went into the kitchen. Moments later, she bought out Tuscan-braised short ribs, baked macaroni and cheese, and an oven roasted vegetable medley made with baby red potatoes, onions, celery, asparagus, and carrots. The different aromas that wafted through my nostrils caused my stomach to talk back.

When the chef walked away, we wasted no time digging into our meal. For a good solid eight minutes all you heard was our forks hitting the plates.

"Why are you single? You are a beautiful person inside and out. You have a good head on your shoulders. Any man would want you."

"That is true. Any man can want me, but the gag is that I must want them too. The men I have come across only have wanted one thing, and that is something that I'm not giving to just anybody.

"Hmm. I see. So, you're the type that has the ninety day rule?"

"Absolutely not. But - "

"Waiting on marriage?" he asked, raising an eyebrow.

"No. I'm - "

"So, what's the issue? You want to make sure that he is the right one?"

Laughing, I nodded and responded, "Yes, I am. I am a virgin and I want to make sure that the person that I do give that to is someone special and someone that I see myself with for a long while."

Clearing his throat, Dominic sat up and spoke. "I guess I came along at the right moment. Could that be the reason why your last relationship didn't work out?"

Sipping my wine, I shrugged my shoulders and answered, "Possibly."

That was one road I didn't want to go down. The thing I had with Mark, I didn't consider that to be a relationship. The one before Mark was my last relationship, and that ended horribly. I allowed myself to be open with a man and emotionally was dragged to hell and back. I loved this man more than anything in this cruel world. He was my peace at the end of a long day, but he was also the reason why I went back to living with my mother. He finessed me something good.

I had met Mike just as I began college. From there we were inseparable. Two years passed and we were still together, and that's when I started to get mysterious phone calls from women saying that they had been with Mike. I was so stupidly in love that he would tell me that they were lying and assure me that he had eyes only on me. That was until one day, a woman called me and told me that she was his wife, that she didn't know what I had going on with her husband. She was certifiably crazy and would more than happily catch a charge behind her man. I wasn't a pussy by any means, but at that time I was getting my shit together and I had a lot to lose. I was working, stacking my account, and going to school. Mike had been away on what he called a business trip and wasn't answering his calls. Keana suggested that we pop up at the apartment he had out in Troy.

Two o' clock in the morning, we pulled up to 432 7th Avenue. The lights were off but in one of the rooms, you could tell that the TV was on. The building door was always un-locked, so gaining access to the building was a guaranteed success.

As we approached his apartment door, we heard arguing. It was Mike's voice, of course, and he was yelling at someone, telling them that they should have never done what they did. Hearing enough, I banged on the door as if I was the police. There was some scrambling going on before the locks were undone.

"What are you doing here, babe?" Mike asked through the crack in the door, like he was hiding something.

"I could ask you the same thing, being that you are sup-posed to be on a business trip. I came to speak with you about something that has been weighting heavy on my spirit."

"Can it wait until tomorrow, babe? I was just about to go to bed for work in the morning. I got in not too long ago."

Keana looked at me and I looked back at her. She moved away from the door and raised her leg, smashing her foot into the door, causing the door to smack Mike in his face. Instinc-tively, Mike let the door go and his hands flew to his face, which gave us the opportunity to get inside the apartment. This nigga had the audacity to have this female sitting on the couch. I wanted to fight, but instead, my heart broke right there into a million pieces. The tears that poured down my face were uncontrollable and the smirk this bitch wore on her face only made things worse. I did nothing but turn my ass around and leave the apartment. A few days later, I went into the bank to withdrawal a couple of dollars, only to find out that this fool had cleaned out both my savings and checking account. After that, I sank into a deep depression, causing me to move back with my mama and start all over again.

"Are you okay?" Dominic asked me.

"Huh? Oh, yeah. I'm okay. Just thought about the fuck shit that nigga did to me. But to answer your question, he broke my heart in unimaginable ways and cleaned out my accounts. I haven't heard from him or seen him again," I answered.

"You got to be more careful with your information. You can't give that type of information out."

"That's the crazy part. I didn't give him any information. He must have went snooping. But I'm done with talking about that. Let's finish enjoying this night and let's toast to new beginnings."

Dominic agreed with me and clinked his glass against mine.

For the remainder of the night we got to know each other, enjoyed wine, and got up a few times to dance. Dominic made sure that I enjoyed my night, and he definitely earned some brownie points for that.

Chapter Four

You've broken down and tired
Of living on a merry go round
And you can't find the fighter
But I see it in you so we gonna
Walk it out

Cheryl

Being able to see my one and only child walk across the stage with a Bachelor's degree ranked number two in my happiest moments. Giving birth to Mah'lani was number one. Being a single parent wasn't the easiest thing to do and several times I wanted to give up. No matter how many times I've felt that way, I still did what I had to do for my baby because she didn't ask to be here. I knew that I had to because of her sorry-ass daddy up and leaving me.

The relationship I had with Malcolm was magical. After two years of being together, I found out I was pregnant with Mah'lani. We were happy, and I thought bringing Mah'lani into this world would brighten our lives together. I was wrong. One day when he had gotten home, I had dinner laid out for him, prepared to tell him the good news. We sat down to eat and everything in me wanted to wait to tell him, but anxiety got the best of me and I blurted it out as soon as the tips of his fingers touched his fork.

Malcolm looked at me and scratched his head. I know I looked a plumb fool with the smile that was on my face as he sat there confused. He calmly told me that I couldn't have Mah'lani. When I asked why not, he simply told me that he was married and had children already. The pieces that my heart broke into couldn't even be explained. From that day on,

I didn't hear or see from him. That was the day I vowed to make sure that my daughter would have the best life possible, even if I felt like I couldn't do it.

"Ms. Carter, your ride is here," my nurse spoke, interrupting my thoughts, I swiped the tears from my face and gathered my things. As I walked out to the waiting area, I saw that Keana was standing there with tissues in her hands and her face was puffy and red.

"Mama Cheryl, are you okay?" she asked, rushing over to me.

"For now, yes."

"What happened? Do you need me to call Mah'lani?"

"No. She's out enjoying herself and she deserves this. I will tell her when I think the time is right. Let's keep this between us, Keana."

"Yes, of course."

"I was diagnosed with aggressive stage three lung cancer. I was exposed to radon in my teen years and found out last year that I had it."

Keana's tears welled in her eyes as she looked at me. Dropping my things on the chair close to me, I grabbed Keana into a tight hug. She was like a daughter to me, and I knew the pain that she was feeling. If Keana reacted this way, I could only imagine how Mah'lani would react. The thought of Mah'lani being out in this world without me broke my heart. Sure, she had Keana and her family, but I know, God forbid, if something was to happen to me, Mah'lani would lose her mind. The next few months would be touch and go and I had to make sure that all of my affairs were in order.

***

Waking up in the morning had become the worst thing to happen to me as of lately. It'd been a week since I broke the news to Keana and I still had yet to tell Mah'lani what was going on. She was the happiest that I'd seen her in a long time. This young man that she had met had my baby on cloud nine and to deliver this bad news…I just couldn't bring myself to do it.

I sat up in my bed in a coughing fit. I reached to the night stand for a Kleenex, thinking it was mucus, but it was, in fact, a glob of blood. My heart dropped into my lap. As I wiped my lips, I heard knocking on my bedroom door and Mah'lani walked in.

"Hey, Mama, I was just coming to let you know that I was headed to work. I heard you coughing. Are you okay? You need some water?" my baby asked me.

"Yes, your old mama is okay. I'll grab some water. You take your behind to work before you're late."

"You might be coming down with a cold. Could be from kissing on that piece of chocolate you had over here," Mah'lani cracked.

I couldn't help but join in with laughter.

"Take your ass to work. I'm cooking tonight so if you want to, bring that dusty nigga that got your panties all twisted over."

Mah'lani's bottom lip dropped and her voice got high-pitched. "Mama, why he got to be a dusty nigga?"

"Because I said so. Now get to work."

I watched as Mah'lani walked over to me and placed a kiss on my forehead. She told me that she loved me and switched her ass up out of my room. When it was safe for me to do so, I allowed the tears to spill from my eyes.

Mah'lani

Lunch time couldn't come any faster. I was having a girls' lunch with Keana right before I was to go out in the field with Clarissa. I needed to spill the beans to Keana that my mama wanted to meet Dominic. I didn't know what we were doing just yet so I couldn't call him my boyfriend, so I opted to use the word "man friend". We were meeting at Atho's restaurant, a Greek restaurant in Albany. As I made my way to the spit, Dominic called me and a smile spread across my face. I answered, making sure that my phone was connected to my Bluetooth.

"Good afternoon, beautiful. How's your day going?" Dominic's voice boomed through the speakers.

"Hey there yourself, handsome. My day is going well, and yours?"

"Amazing, now that I hear your voice."

"Aw shucks! You just trying to earn some brownie points." I giggled.

"Nah, I'm on some for real shit, baby girl. I could be having the worst day of my life and hearing your voice just makes it all better. You have no idea how bad my day has been."

"Aww, tell me about it."

"I'd rather not, shorty. It's nothing you have to worry your pretty little head about. Besides that, what your pretty ass got planned for tonight?"

"Ooh, I'm glad that you asked because it damn sure slipped my mind. How would you like to join me and my mama for dinner? She requested that you be there."

Dominic chuckled heatedly and answered, "Oh shit! I thought it would have been too soon to meet your moms."

"Don't worry, I thought so too, but she asked and I've got no business telling my mama no. So that means you can't say no."

"Okay, okay. I got you, love. I can't tell your pretty ass no anyhow. And what kind of man would I be if I turned down the woman who gave birth to my future wife?"

My cheeks flushed red and yes, I was too old get all googly-eyed when a nigga made promises too soon, but it felt good to hear it. Absentmindedly, I pulled into the parking lot at Atho's and told Dominic that I would text him the time to come on over and I gave him the address.

Today I was looking scrumptious in a blush pink pencil skirt, a white short-sleeved V-neck blouse, and just in case I got cold, I had the matching blush pink blazer. On my feet were nude-colored pumps that buckled at the ankle and had crystal flowers on the strap. My hair and makeup were slayed to the gods and nobody or they nappy headed-ass mama could tell me different. I parked and got out of my car, strutting like a runway model. Keana was already waiting on me.

"You been here for long?" I asked Keana as I approached the table.

Keana's eyes wandered from the menu up to me and she began to smile. She said, "Okay, bitch. I see you looking the way you look. You lucky we in this place or I would have yelled that shit at the top of my lungs. You hear me?"

"Thank God, 'cause we both know your loud ass could wake the dead," I spoke, taking my seat.

"Fuck you. And to answer your question, no, I wasn't here for long. But you know that we come here so often that they came right over and took our order."

"What do you mean, took our order? How do you know what I want?" I asked, scrunching my nose up.

"We get the same thing all of the time. Grilled lamb chops, Greek salad topped with grilled octopus, even though it's not supposed to be on it, and we could possibly be disrespecting their culture, a side of stuffed grape leaves made with both lamb and beef. Oh, let's not forget our frappes. It never changes, and I doubt that it will because you are afraid to try new things."

"Bitch, fuck you."

Keana placed her hand on her chest, acting as if she was offended. She stated, "Such language."

Giggles erupted from us as our waiter began to bring us our food. After making small chit chat, I decided to cut the small talk and tell her about my mom wanting to meet Dominic. When I told Keana, her facial expressions changed so much and so fast that I couldn't read them.

"You mean to tell me that Mama Cheryl voluntarily asked you to bring Dominic to dinner?" Keana asked, just as shocked as I had been.

"She called him a dusty nigga and said that he had my panties twisted. Child, my mama is something else."

"Girl, you act like I don't know that. Remember when we called ourselves being grown and wanted your mama to meet my dude, um – oh shit, what was his name?" Keana spoke, snapping her fingers.

"I think it was Jared. And hell yeah, I remember. She dragged your ass through the dirt with all of the embarrassing things you've done." I laughed.

"Mama Cheryl wrong for that, but you know what? I'm glad she did, because she was trying to show me that he wasn't shit. Remember when I went to that nigga's house and after he swore up and down that nothing was going on with his baby mother, I walked in on them fucking? Trifling Negros had the nerves to be humping in the living room while they motherfucking baby was in the play pen watching *Sesame Street*."

I did remember that day. That was the day I met Mike's trifling ass. After Keana caught them, she left without saying a word, came and picked me up, and we went back. I guess they thought that shit was sweet because they went right back to fucking. Jared knew that Keana had the damn key so for him to fuck his baby mother, knowing that Keana was bound to pop up, was beyond me. It was like Royal Rumble when we had gotten back to Jared's place and Keana wouldn't let up. Eventually, the fight spilled onto the street and Jared had had enough. He went to grab Keana off his baby mother, but he was going for her hair and I lost it. With all my might, I pushed him off her and he ended up catching himself from falling and pushed me. I stumbled, and that's when Mike stepped in.

My ringing phone brought me back to reality and Clarissa's name popped up on the screen. Sliding my finger across the screen, I rolled my eyes while answering. "Hello."

"I know that you are out at lunch, but how fast can you meet me a Parkview Apartments?"

"In about fifteen minutes."

"Meet me there. This is an emergency case."

"I'm on my way," I said as I hung up. Cutting my lunch with Keana short, I gave her my half of the bill, which she didn't take. I threw it on the table and ran out. This was my first time going out on the field, and I was super excited, although I didn't know what was going to happen.

I met Clarissa in the parking lot and she brought me up to speed with what was going on.

"Child's father hasn't seen the child in a few months due to the child's mother not allowing him. There is a court order in place, and obviously she violated the order. We were called in because of the cops giving us a call. Let's head on up," Clarissa spoke.

I was nervous as hell and I didn't know what to expect. After entering the building, we took the elevator up to the tenth floor and walked down the hallway. There was a horrid smell in the hallway that I couldn't place, but it was a mixture of old rotten food, dirty clothes that'd been sitting for weeks, urine, and something moldy. As we got closer to the door, I noticed that it was open, and the smell was coming from that apartment. My stomach began to turn, and I almost lost the food that I had just consumed.

The inside of the apartment was disgusting. Food was all over the place: on the couches, the tables in the living room, pieces on the floor. Clothes were all over the place in one room, there was spoiled milk, and cigarette butts sat on the tables as well. Moving further into the apartment, I saw that trash lined the halls, and stains adorned the walls like it was extra paint. There were only two bedrooms and the master bedroom was just the beginning. I wanted to kick this lady's ass for having this apartment this disgusting. Mountains of old food wrappers and soda bottles came up to damn near my shins. Clothes yet again were piled up high, and there were paper plates with old residue food on them.

"Are you okay?" Clarissa asked, looking at me.

"Yeah. I'm just trying not to lose my food."

"Trust me, I know. I've seen worse."

The whole apartment was fucked up. We had to make sure where we were stepping, and I should have dressed better for the occasion. I knew we were going to be out on the field, only because Clarissa let me know we were going to do a home visit, and I doubt this was it because she would have told me. We finally made it into the other room, where everyone had congregated. The mother was sitting on the bed with the child, who was about four years old, the father stood off to the side in the corner with his hand covering his nose. Two police officers were in another corner, standing and acting as if the smell didn't bother them.

Officer One began to talk. "Dad has tried multiple times to get a visit for months now and Mom has denied him. Upon his arrival, she wouldn't allow him entry into the apartment. He said that he noticed the smell coming through the door as they argued, and that's when he called us. Which is why you guys are here."

Clarissa nodded her head and then turned to the mother. She began to speak. "Your name is Leslie, correct?"

She nodded.

"Okay, ma'am. I hate to admit this to you, but we are going to have to place Malayshia into her dad's care, upon making sure that he has enough space and that his apartment is clean. This is an unsanitary living environment for not only your daughter, but you as well. This apartment is a health hazard. Mah'lani, get on the phone with code," Clarissa spoke softly.

"Y'all are not taking my baby," Leslie stated.

"Leslie, I'm sorry, we have to because of the conditions that the apartment is in. You can always get her back, but she has to go with her dad right now."

The father jumped in and spoke, "She's not getting her back. I'm going to make sure of that. My place is big enough for me to hold four families and it is always immaculately clean."

Officer Two turned to the father and let him know that the next time he said something, he was going to have to leave the premises. As I hung up my phone with code, I noticed that Leslie had been holding her hand behind her back. I cautiously walked over toward Malayshia. I wasn't even two steps closer to her when Leslie brandished a knife and held it up against Malayshia's throat. My mouth dropped, and mayhem erupted. The officer drew their guns, the dad began to scream obscenities, and Clarissa and I stood there frozen. Officer One radioed for back up and finally, Clarissa's feet began to move. She grabbed the dad by the arm and rushed him out of the room.

Leslie continued to yell that no one was taking her child while Malayshia cried. My heart ached at what was in front of me.

"Everybody calm down for two seconds!" I shouted. The room got quiet, except for Malayshia's cries. I continued, "Listen, Leslie, I understand that you don't want to be separated from your baby girl, but look at your environment. If you want to make things better for you and Malayshia, you must do things differently. You must start over and make things right, but you can't do this. I know that you love that little girl more than life itself, but the way you are scaring her will always be etched into her mind. This isn't healthy for either one of y'all. Put the knife down, Leslie, and let Malayshia go with her dad. This is the best option."

Leslie looked at me. I saw the pain in her eyes. She was hurting, and only she knew why. My heart ached for her. I wanted to grab her into my arms and just hold her to let her know that everything was going to be okay, even if I knew that it wouldn't. She was going to jail after this. The tears landed on her shirt as she shook her head.

"No. I have been through hell and back trying to have her. I almost died on the table. And y'all think that y'all can just come in here and just give her to her dumb-ass dad."

"Leslie, help me to make me see that this makes sense. The way that you are living is in an unsanitary environment. You'd rather kill or harm your child, the one you almost died having, might I add, all because you don't want to see her with her dad. That must be the most selfish thing that I have heard all day," I spoke, all professionalism going out of the window. I had to check myself because I was 2.5 seconds away from fighting her dumb ass.

"Do you have any kids?" she asked in between hiccups and crying.

"No, I don't."

"So how could you possibly even come close to under-standing my situation? Her father didn't want me to have her when he found out I was pregnant with her. I had to take him to court for him to do for her. And only then did he start picking her up, buying her clothes, and things of that nature."

Placing my hands on my hips, I was full on pissed. I opened my mouth and as best as I could, talked calmly. "You have life fucked up. I get that you're hurt and in pain. I get you want to protect your daughter. But look around you, Leslie. This house is downright nasty. You are sitting here with a knife to your daughter's throat! All for what? Because you don't want her dad, who is making up for all the shit you had to put him through to get him to step up, to have temporary custody so you can get your shit together?"

Clarissa walked back inside of the room, followed by more officers with their guns drawn. Clarissa said, "Mah'lani, why are you doing all of this yelling?"

Without saying a word, I watched as Leslie shook as she removed the knife from Malayshia's neck. Leslie dropped the knife to the floor, and I rushed in to grab Malayshia and bring her to her father. What I did was super unprofessional but, in that moment, I did what I had to do. I'd take it if Clarissa yelled at me or wrote me up, but I was only trying to make sure that everyone left that situation alive.

"Thank you so much," Malayshia's dad said to me.

Minutes later, the police came out with Leslie in hand-cuffs. I shook my head because I knew that she wasn't going to see her child until she was well into her teen years, damn near almost to adulthood. Getting off work and going to have a drink was the only thing on my mind.

Clarissa walked up to me with disappointment in her eyes. "What was that, Mah'lani?" she asked.

"Clarissa, I honestly don't know. What she was saying made absolutely no sense."

"I get that, and that can't happen again. But today, I'm glad that you did it. If you didn't, she would have killed that baby and herself. I know this is heavy for you. You can have the rest of the day off. You did good, Mah'lani," she expressed.

"Thank you," I responded and made my way home.

***

At seven o'clock that night, Dominic was knocking on the door and my stomach was turning in knots. The table was already set with stewed chicken and potatoes, cornbread, rice and peas, and steamed broccoli. My mother got fancy and had poured our glasses full of Dom Perignon Rose.

"I am not the parent who's going to sit here and ask you what your intentions are with my daughter. Y'all grown and I'm pretty sure that y'all know the do's and don'ts when in a relationship. The only thing that I have to say would be treat my daughter right. She deserves that much. If you can do that, then you're good in my book," my mama expressed.

"Ms. Carter, you have my word on that," Dominic responded with a smile on his face.

"Then in that case, you can call me Mama Cheryl."

The night went by with ease, and not only did Dominic win my mama over, but he officially won me over.

Chapter Five

Six months later

Just gonna stand there and watch me burn
But that's alright, because I like the way it hurts
Just gonna stand there and hear me cry
But that's alright, because I love the way you lie

My favorite time of the year had arrived. Snow was slowly falling, and my closet was filling up with gifts. "Jingle Bells" had been on rotation since the day after Thanksgiving. My relationship with Dominic was spectacular. On the weekends when I was not working we were in a different city in New York, enjoying the festivities in that city. My life at this moment was perfect and I couldn't imagine my life differently.

The weekend before Christmas, Dominic wanted to stay home. We weren't spending Christmas together because he had business to take care of in Memphis. At first, I side-eyed him, until he showed me papers from his lawyer that showed he was going to buy a building for real estate. He was about his business, and that's what I loved about him.

Friday had hit, and I was ready to go home and wind down with a drink. My feet were killing me, and a nice hot bath was on the agenda. Dominic was out in the streets making sure that his businesses were running smoothly, and I knew that he wouldn't come in until late. On the weekends, I spent time at his house. He had given me the key three months prior and I happily used it every weekend.

After climbing the stairs to his front door, I checked the mailbox while laughing at Keana's text telling me about her day at work.

"Girl, you better leave them kids alone at that group home. Don't you know that they will straight jump you?" I laughed into the phone. I inserted the keys and entered the house, losing my life in the process.

"Ahh!" I screamed.

"Mah'lani! What happened? You good? What's going on?" Keana asked over the phone, concerned.

Trying to regain my breath and my soul, I answered, "Yeah, I'm good. Dominic just scared the shit out of me. I'm gonna call you back."

"Okay, girl. And tell him to cut his shit," she spoke.

I told her that I would and hung up. After placing my items on the couch, I walked into Dominic's open arms. *Damn, he smells good,* I thought to myself. He was wearing my favorite scent, Mr. Burberry. He knew that every time that he wore it, it did something to me.

"I'm sorry for scaring you. I was just trying to surprise you."

"Surprise me? Why?"

Dominic put his hands in mine and looked me in my eyes. I tried to read his expression, but I couldn't. Maybe 'cause his ass had smoked and his eyes were barely slits. Dominic licked his lips in an LL Cool J manner and began to speak, "I had to move my trip to this weekend. I know it's last minute, but there is a slight misunderstanding down in St. Louis."

"St. Louis?" I questioned. *I know when he told me about this, he told me that he was going to be in Memphis,* I thought to myself.

"Yeah. Remember the real estate deal I told you about?"

"Yes, of course."

"The seller is trying to back out, but I really need this location. I have an idea of opening a soul food restaurant in remembrance of my mother."

"Speaking of, you rarely speak about your parents."

Dominic sighed and moved off of the couch and dragged his hand across his face. Dominic had briefly told me that his dad's mom was a crackhead. She passed two years ago and that was all that I knew.

"I don't speak about them, because there is nothing to speak upon. I've told you all that I think that you should know," Dominic responded.

"You never told me how your mom was. For me to get to know you, I feel like I should know about your parents."

"Mah'lani, please just drop it. I'm trying to have an amazing weekend with you because next week you're working, and I must prepare for my trip. I'm already feeling bad about having to go Christmas weekend. This was supposed to be our first Christmas together -"

"But wait, you just said that you were going this weekend. What are you talking about? I am confused right now."

Dominic's face remained expressionless as he looked at me. What he said next almost made me fly off the handle. He said, "I have to be down there again next weekend as well, to make sure everything goes well after this weekend. Anything could happen from the time that I leave down there on Sunday."

I didn't outright want to call him a liar, but my radar was up. After all, he did have a point. So whether he was going down both weekends or not, the fact remained that we weren't going to be spending Christmas together. So maybe, just maybe, I could drop it this one time.

"Okay. I apologize, Dominic. I just want to enjoy my last night with you. Obviously, you wanted to do the same thing because I know you want to be out there making sure your businesses are running right."

Dominic reached for my hand and pulled me towards his lap. As I sat down, he gripped the back of my neck and pulled me towards him to places kisses on my neck. His beard tickled my face and neck as my panties became moist. He knew just what to do to make me feel this way and I must admit, I commend him for waiting on me. We came damn near close to Dominic taking my virginity, but before things got too heavy, he would always stop because he didn't want me to feel like he was forcing me into anything. Little did he know, I didn't know how much longer I was going to be able to hold on to my purity.

"Since you put it that way, let's go in the kitchen," Dominic whispered as he pushed his pelvis onto my butt, letting me know that his dick had become bricked up.

Biting my lip, I went into the kitchen. In there, on the table, sat baked macaroni and cheese, stir fry vegetables, and fried chicken. I smiled and turned to Dominic. This was the first time he had cooked for me.

"Yes, I cooked. I told you that it was going to be a surprise." Dominic smirked.

I walked up to Dominic and wrapped my arms around his neck. I looked him in his eyes and thanked him with a kiss. Dominic reached around my waist and with both hands, grabbed my ass cheeks.

"Mmm. Keep on, you might just get a shot of this tonight," I moaned into his ear.

Pausing his kisses, he unbuttoned my pants and slipped his hands into my panties. Instantly, his fingers were coated with my juices. He rubbed his index and middle finger between my slit.

"You love to talk shit, don't you?" he spoke into my ear. He roughly turned me around and walked to the counter.

I was against the counter and he was against me. My breathing became heavy as his fingers twirled around in my box.

"Mmm...don't stop," I moaned.

Turning me back around, Dominic pulled my pants down and placed me onto the counter. Dominic bit his bottom lip sexually, placing my titties into the palms of his hands. His fingers slid between my other set of lips yet again, causing my juices to flow onto the counter. Dominic pulled his pants down, massaging his dick through his boxers.

"Lean your back against the cabinets and bend your legs to plant your feet on the counter. I want to see that pretty pussy," Dominic spoke in somewhat of a growl. Dominic was a freak and I loved every single minute of it.

I watched Dominic stroke himself as I replaced my fingers where his were. Dominic began to tell me all the things he wanted to do to me and I closed my eyes to picture all the things he said. This was how we got off, as much as I was tired of doing that, and I knew he was too. As far as I knew, he wasn't fucking any other chick, but I wouldn't blame him if he was. If roles were reversed, I know that as a male, I wouldn't be waiting around for some pussy.

Moments later, I coated my fingers with my juices and climbed down off the counter. Tonight was the night that Dominic was getting it. I could not wait any longer. My hips swayed as I walked over to Dominic sexually. I took my shirt and bra off. My eyes never left Dominic's as I grabbed both of my breasts and pinched my nipples in between my fingers.

As I got closer to Dominic, his head leaned back against the wall. Dropping to my knees, I licked my lips and wrapped my hands around the base of his dick. I eased him into my mouth and moistened his dick with my saliva. Slow and steady was my pace and how he liked it. His fingers ran through my hair as the tip of his dick tickled my tonsils. His balls were nestled in my warm hands, waiting for my mouth.

"Sssss! Damn, girl," Dominic hissed.

My eyes immediately went to his, and his eyes were rolling to the back of his head. After slipping his dick from my mouth, I placed his balls into my mouth and softly sucked on them while stroking his dick. His toes curled, and I knew he was about to cum. I took him out of my mouth, kissed the tip of his dick, and walked away. When I got upstairs to the bedroom, I knew that Dominic was planning on taking my virginity tonight. On the bed were rose petals, on the nightstand was a bottle of champagne in an ice bucket, and there was lingerie on the bed. My mouth dropped, and I moved closer to the bed.

"Tonight, I wanted it to be special. I've known since the moment I met you that you were going to be mine. I've never fallen for someone so fast and I must admit, Mah'lani, that it feels damn good. You came into my life at a point where everything was chaotic. I love you, Mah'lani, and when the time is right, we will make it official and make things as one," Dominic whispered in my ear from behind me.

My heart pounded in my chest because he was right. We fell for one another fast as hell and I was just happy that we felt the same way mutually. Dominic's strong arms wrapped around me while he placed kisses on my neck. His hands roamed freely over my body.

"I love you too, Dominic," I replied.

I turned around to face him and with ease, he picked me up and I wrapped my legs around his waist. Our lips immediately met, and our tongues danced. He walked over to the bed and laid me down on it, spreading my legs wide enough for him to lay in between them. His tongue wrapped around my clit as he sucked on it, bringing me into instant pleasure. It was my turn for my eyes to roll to the back of my head. My legs shook and the only noises that were heard were my moans and his face sliding around in my juices.

"Dominic, you're going to make me cum," I squealed.

"Nah, don't do that yet," Dominic requested as he came from between my legs and climbed the length of body.

His lips met mine yet again, taking me straight to ecstasy. I felt his dick bumping against my pussy and realized that this shit was about happen. Dominic's hands interlocked into mine as he left a trail of kisses down my chest onto my breasts, sucking each one into his mouth. I'm sure that there was a puddle by now under my body.

"Is it going to hurt? Because I've heard that it is painful," I stammered.

Chuckling, Dominic shook his head and responded, "Babe, for every girl, it's different. While some may think that it hurts, you might think otherwise. But one thing for sure is that it all ends up pleasurable."

Dominic got up from the bed and grabbed a bottle. I noticed that it was KY Jelly and I sat up. I asked, "Do you really think that you need that? It feels like a puddle is under my ass. Just get over here, Dominic."

He nodded his head and came back to the bed and placed his body on top of mine. Dominic grabbed my leg and placed it over his waist. He grabbed his dick and slowly guided his dick to my hole. My body tensed up as I felt slight pressure. Dominic slowly moved in and out of me and he was right. I moved my hips in tune with his and dug my nails into his skin. He placed his head in the crook of my neck and softly bit into my flesh.

"Ooh shit!" I moaned. My pussy was wetter than it had ever been.

"My God! Your pussy is fucking amazing, babe," Dominic confessed. He flipped me over onto my stomach and reentered me, causing me to scream out in pleasure. Using his hands, he spread my ass cheeks and watched his dick go in and out of me. Moments later things got a little heavy as he pounded my box deeply while pulling my hair.

"Mmm, shit!" I moaned, wondering why I had waited so long to do this.

Dominic pressed his body against mine, continuing his stroke, and he whispered, "You don't need another nigga for nothing. Do you understand? This pussy is mine. If I even think you looking at another nigga, I will hurt you. Do we have an understanding, Mah'lani?"

"Mmm, yes! Dominic, yes, this is yours. Oh my God! I'm cumming!" I yelled as I felt my juices coat his dick and stick to the inside of my legs. What I thought was Dominic talking dirty, I should have known was a red flag.

Dominic kept me on my toes for the remainder of the night. Dinner ended up getting cold and in the wee hours of the morning, we had to heat the food up.

While I slept, Dominic stayed up to pack his things and get ready for his flight. It wasn't sitting well with me that he had lied about where he was going. He did travel a lot, so it could have been a simple mistake. I'd leave it alone for the meantime and push it to the back of my mind until I needed to bring it back up again.

At seven o' clock in the morning, I woke up to the rain pounding against the window. Lightning stroked across the sky and thunder shook the house. My body was in a lot of pain and between my legs it was super sticky. Flashes of the way Dominic handled my body made my body warm all over. Having sex with him could have been the best thing that I had done in a long while. Removing the covers from my body, I sat up and reached for my phone that was on the table next to the bed. Dominic had left me a message explaining that he had ordered me some breakfast from Denny's and that it was on top of the stove. He also explained how he left me a gift on the coffee table.

I grabbed my things to get in the shower and afterward, I planned on enjoying my breakfast from Denny's. He also explained how he left me a gift on the coffee table.

As I enjoyed my breakfast of pancakes, sausage, bacon, eggs, and French toast, I watched the cast of *Love and Hip-Hop Atlanta* cut up. A bag from Victoria's Secret sat on the table and remembering that it was my gift, I reached for the bag and looked inside. My mouth dropped as I saw the money that was in the bag. Hundreds were stacked, and it totaled over five thousand dollars.

"What the fuck?" I exclaimed out loud. I picked up my phone and tried calling Dominic, but his phone was going straight to voicemail. Next person I called was my mama.

"Child, what do you want? Ain't you supposed to be enjoying time with your man?" my mother answered her phone.

"I would if he was here. He had to go handle something a little bit earlier than what we thought," I answered.

"Well shit, why didn't you let me know sooner? I would have made plans with you."

"It's okay, Mama. You have a life now with Omar. I'll be fine. I was calling you to ask you for some advice."

"Okay. Go ahead."

"Dominic left me some money. I don't know what to do with it."

"You really need my advice on what to do with a few dollars?"

"Mama, I would hardly say that over five thousand dollars is a few dollars."

The sound of my mother spitting her drink from her mouth caused me to chuckle. She finally spoke. "Whattt?"

"You heard me right, Mama. Do I spend it? Do I save it? What do I do?"

"What you do with it is totally up to you. I'm surprised that you even need to ask what you should do with it. I can tell you, though, that if you think he is going to continue to put that type of money in your hands again, then you should definitely start saving most of it for a rainy day."

"I don't know, Mama. Hold on, Mama, I have a text message coming through," I explained.

Pressing the home button, I dragged down the notification bar and saw that it was Dominic. He had texted me and told me not to hesitate to spend the money, that it made up for him having to leave two weeks in a row. He said that he was going to make sure that even though he was going to miss spending Christmas with me, he was still going to make sure that I had something special under the tree. I couldn't help but smile.

"Okay, Mama, I'm back. That was just Dominic reading my mind. He told me to spend it."

"See? I told you. Oh, and I better have something special under the tree."

"Spoiled much?"

"Spoiled not enough. I made sure that you took your ass to school, made sure that you always had clothes on your back, food in your -"

"Okay, Mama, dang. I get your point," I interrupted. Whenever she wanted something from me, that was her tactic to make me cave in. As usual, it worked. I could practically hear her smiling through the phone.

I wrapped up my phone call with my mother and began to get ready to head to the mall for last minute Christmas shopping. Thanks to Dominic, everyone's gifts would be better than what I would have gotten on my own.

***

Next Saturday – Christmas Day

Snow covered everything outside and it didn't seem like it was letting up. Christmas was my favorite holiday and I'd waited all year just to slip my feet into fuzzy socks and comfy pajamas and sip hot chocolate on the couch with a warm blanket and *A Christmas Story* on the TV. As a child, when I woke up, I would race down the stairs and open every last gift my mother had bought. My mother allowed me to believe in Santa Claus up until I was five, when I was able to understand that Santa Claus wasn't real. That was the only year that I ever disliked my mom. But of course, as I got older, I understood why she did it.

Since Dominic was gone, I was at home with my mama, and I couldn't wait to see her face when she opened her gift. Clad in my fuzzy socks and comfy pajamas, I made my way to the living room. My mother wasn't in the living room, nor the kitchen as she usually would be, so I went to go search for her. My first stop was her room.

Knock! Knock!

"Mama, why aren't you downstairs?" I asked, walking into her room. She was still in bed, under the covers. She didn't respond, which was unusual because she was a light sleeper. *Maybe she was just tired,* I thought. I walked over to the bed and pulled the covers down from her shoulders. I smiled at how peaceful she looked. Looking closer, I noticed that her lips were a weird tint of blue. My heart began to pound in my chest. Touching her face, I found that she was freezing. I touched her neck for a pulse. It was there, but faintly.

"No, no, no! Mama!" I yelled, looking for her phone to call for an ambulance.

"911, what's the address to your emergency?" the dispatcher asked.

"1126 State Street, Schenectady, New York," I said in a shaky voice.

"Ma'am, what is your emergency?"

The tears were relentless. "My mom is barely breathing. Her pulse is weak and she's ice cold."

"Is she responsive?"

"No! Just please hurry and send someone."

"Okay, ma'am. I just need to ask you a few more questions."

When she was done, I tried rolling her onto her back and began CPR. My mind was all over the place and I was almost borderline going into a panic attack.

"Come on, Mama. You can't leave me like this. Not now! I don't know what's wrong, but you cannot go!" I yelled.

There was a banging on the door and I ran to open it. The fire department had arrived first, and I led them into my mother's room. I ran everything down to them, everything that I knew, and then I went to go grab my coat and shoes. By the time I came back, the E.M.T's were taking my mama out on a stretcher. They let me know to follow her in the car. Locking up the house, I jumped in the car and called Keana.

"Merry Christmas, chica," Keana sang into the phone.

"Keana," I whimpered into the phone.

"What's wrong?" Keana answered.

"Meet me at Ellis Hospital. There is something wrong with my mama," I cried.

"Okay, girl. I'll be there."

I hung up the phone and prayed all the way to the hospital. Memories of me and my mom filled my mind. I couldn't lose my mother. I would literally go bananas.

I made it to the hospital just as they were taking my mother out of the ambulance. I followed, spewing a bunch of questions. They held me back and told me to wait until a doctor came to talk to me. Keana and her family came running into the waiting area. When she saw me, Keana ran right into my arms and hugged me tight.

"What's going on? What's wrong with Mama Cheryl?" Keana asked with tears forming in her eyes.

"I don't know. I woke up so that we could open our gifts, but I noticed that she wasn't in the living room or the kitchen, so I went to check in her room. She was barely breathing, she was cold, and had a weak pulse," I cried. I licked my lips and squeezed my hands as if I was wringing them out.

Keana took my hands into hers and pulled me into a hug. She kept apologizing to me. I didn't want to hear anything except that my mama was going to be okay. That God forbid, she had an allergic reaction to something, that it took so long to react that her throat slowly began to close during the night. At least, that was my thinking, whether it made sense or not. When Keana pulled herself away from me, she grabbed my hand and tugged on it, indicating that she wanted to talk to me away from everybody else.

"Keana, I can't think straight. I don't know what I'm going to do."

"I know, and I'm here for you. I need to tell you something."

"Whatever it is, you just have to wait on it."

"No, Mah'lani, this is something that you need to know."

Just then the doctor came out and grabbed our attention. Only he didn't come out on behalf of my mother. Keana caught my attention again and I was becoming quite irritated by it. I wiped my eyes and said, "Whatever it is you have to tell me, it better be more important than my mother lying in that hospital bed, possibly about to die. I'm trying really hard to not take my emotions out on you because you are my best friend, but you need to understand that if it's not about my mom, I couldn't care less right about now."

"Believe me, I wouldn't talk about nothing other than what is going on now."

"You got the floor," I said, looking out of the window.

"Six months ago, the day that you had your first date with Dominic, your mom called me because she hadn't been feeling well. She didn't call you because she didn't want to mess up your date. Anyway, she was at the hospital and, um -"

"Family for Cheryl Carter," the doctor called out.

I left Keana and went to stand in front of him. Keana and her family stood behind me as if they were a shield.

"Yes. I'm her daughter."

"Your mom is stable for the moment. She is sedated and is on oxygen. We have a machine helping her breath, but we don't know how long she will be able to stay this way. We almost lost her trying to stabilize her. Your mother has stage three lung cancer and it's progressing aggressively. At this point in time, it's touch and go."

"My mother has what!" I yelled.

"I'm sorry; you didn't know?" the doctor asked, confused.

"Would I be reacting this way if I did?"

Keana walked closer to me and placed her head on my shoulder. She said, "I was about to tell her."

I turned around so fast that I knocked Keana's hand off my shoulder. My eyes were wide, and her eyes were to the ground, in shame. Confused, I said, "What?"

"I was trying to tell you that before the doctor came out to tell you. Mama Cheryl asked me not to tell you. She wanted to tell you herself."

"Keana, you are my best friend. I don't care what she said. Something like that, you should have told me. If that was Mama Alice or Papa Nate, even if they made me swear on the bible, that is nothing that I would keep from you. Just go Keana."

Keana's tears poured down her eyes as they pleaded with me. "Mah'lani, please let me stay and be here for you."

"No! I don't even want to look at you right now. Friends don't keep secrets away from each other," I said and I walked away.

I followed the doctor down the hallway to the room that held my mother. I couldn't help but feel betrayed by Keana. Granted, at stage three there wasn't much that I could have done, but at least I would have gotten a heads up about how much time I would have left with her. The pain in my heart was unmeasurable. This couldn't be happening.

The beeping sounds from the machines made this all real for me. My mother was covered up to her chest in blankets, and the machine that was helping her breathe wheezed with each fall of her chest.

"Mama, I whispered. I fell into the chair that was next to her bed and wept. My chest ached something terrible. I cried until I couldn't anymore. My mother needed to shake this. Or at least wake up so that I could do all that I could to help her get better.

My phone buzzed in my pocket, indicating that I had a phone call coming through. I turned it off and gave my mother all my attention.

<u>Three days later</u>

The words "no progress" kept ringing in my head. That was the diagnosis that my mom was given every day since she had been admitted. The third day, when I arrived at the hospital, I finally turned my phone on. There was a slew of messages from Keana and Dominic. I bypassed Keana's messages and looked at Dominic's. They went from lovely messages wishing me a Merry Christmas, to worry, and then they were aggressive messages, insinuating that I had gone behind his back and fucked another dude while he was away. My head dropped because at that moment, I didn't want to deal with that. I knew that I had to call him to let him know what was going on."

"So now you want to call? How dare you go out and spread your legs to any ole nigga? You think that I wasn't going to find out?" Dominic spat through the phone with disgust lacing his voice.

"I didn't, Dominic. I shouldn't have turned my phone off, but I only did because - "

"Because what? You got a taste of dick and you wanted to go spread it wide for some other nigga?"

"Dominic, my head is pounding, and I just need for you to listen to me. Can you please do that? I don't want to argue."

Dominic paused, contemplating on if he was going to listen or not. Finally, after several seconds he spoke. "Go ahead."

"My mother was near death. I found her on Christmas morning, cold and not responding. I am still in the hospital with her and if you listen close enough, you can hear the beeping of the machines. I just found out that she has aggressive stage three cancer. Oh, and the worst part is that Keana knew about it for six months and failed to mention it because my mom made her promise not to tell me." I sniffled as I broke down crying again.

"I am so sorry, babe. I-I-I don't know what to say."

"You don't have to say nothing. I'm sorry for shutting my phone off. I should have at least reached out to you to let you know something."

"What hospital are you at?"

"I'm at Ellis."

"I'm on my way."

"No, Dominic. I know you have a lot to take care of to get ready for your trip."

"I don't want to hear that. I'm on my way. All that other shit isn't important," Dominic stated and hung the phone up.

I placed my hands on my mother and prayed harder than I ever had. Knowing that Dominic was on his way to come and sit with me eased my mind. Dealing with this alone had taken a major toll on my body and mind. Keana should have been here with me, but finding out that she knew hurt me to my core. Eventually, I would forgive her, but for now, it was too fresh.

Mimi

Chapter Six

Still can't believe you're gone
Give anything to hear half your breath
I know you still living life, after death

The Lord must have been feeling my pain. The heavy down-pour of the rain was my soul crying. I never thought this day was coming so soon. Dominic went all out to make sure that my mother was laid to rest in the very best. Her casket was white trimmed in gold, and gold satin lined the inside of the casket. Red and white roses sat on pedestals around the casket. She was dressed in a white pantsuit, her hair was in curls, and her makeup was immaculate. She looked like an angel and I couldn't have been happier that Dominic did my mama right.

The day that she died was the day after Dominic offered to come sit with me at the hospital. The sound of her taking her last breath repeated in my head every day since. If it wasn't for Dominic and Keana, I honestly didn't know how I was going to push through. I had no parts in planning my mom's funeral. I wasn't competent enough to do so. I called out of work for a leave of absence and sulked in my mother's bed until the day of her funeral.

Keana came over a few hours before the funeral and helped me get ready. She helped me get dressed in black slacks, a white blouse, and a black blazer. My hair was pulled back and I wasn't in the mood for makeup.

"Keana, I'm sorry for flipping out on you," I said. I was standing up against the sink, trying to calm my nerves by drinking a cup of coffee.

"Girl, bye. You don't have to apologize. You were just re-acting the way any person would have. After I realized that, I was good. I knew you would come around sooner than later. It just sucks that it had to be this way," Keana expressed.

"I miss her already and we haven't even put her in the ground yet."

"We all miss her, Lani, but we now have our very own guardian angel."

"You're right." I placed my cup in the sink and placed my shoes on my feet.

Dominic walked into the house looking dapper in a black piece suit with a smoky grey and white bow tie.

"Ladies, are you ready?" he asked.

Both Keana and I nodded as we followed Dominic out of the house and into the limo. The ride was quiet besides the gospel music that the driver was playing. We arrived at the church fifteen minutes later, and I couldn't bring myself to walk up the church steps. Dominic walked behind me and placed his hands on my shoulders.

"I don't know if I can do this," I whimpered. Keana held my hand, squeezing it to let me know that everything would be okay.

"Yes, you can, babe. Keana and I will be by your side every step of the way," Dominic spoke. He grabbed my hand and tugged on it slightly so that I could follow him.

And I did. Into the church, stuck in tunnel vision. That's pretty much how the funeral went for me. I heard people crying, I heard the preacher, and I heard the choir singing, but I was just stuck. Not a single tear slid down my face, nor did I get up to view her body. I wasn't ready to let her go. From that moment on, it was a blur. It didn't hit me until we were at the burial. It was just Keana and her family, Dominic, and myself at the burial. We stood around the gravesite, placing flowers onto her casket as it got lowered. The rain had let up and the sun was beginning to shine, an indication to me that my mother's soul was able to go through the pearly gates. The sound of footsteps sloshing behind us caught my attention. I turned around and there was a family of four walking up behind us. Mother, father, and two teenaged daughters. The guy was holding flowers and all their faces held sadness.

"Can I help you?" I asked as they got closer, causing everybody to turn in their direction.

"We were just coming to pay our respects to Cheryl," the guy spoke. He was a handsome older man with skin almost the same color as mine. He was tall, just shy of 6'5", with light brown eyes.

"Thank you. How did you know my mom?"

The guy looked at me, then at his wife, and back to me again. He said, "We were good friends."

For some reason, I didn't quite believe him, but I turned back around to see that the groundskeeper had begun to lower my mother into the ground. I dropped to my knees and wailed as if I was a child again who was not getting what I wanted. Keana and Dominic tried to hold me up, but they couldn't. I wanted nothing more than for my mother to jump out of that casket and tell me that I had been punked. The guy who came with his family looked at me with pity as they threw their flowers on top of her casket and walked away. Dominic pulled me away five minutes later, placed me in the back of the limo, and went back to talk to Keana. Looking out of the window at them, I noticed the guy walking back up to them and talking with them. They couldn't see me watching, but their attention was directed towards me for a few moments. Dominic and Keana made their way back to the limos and Keana joined her family while Dominic joined me.

"What did that guy want?" I asked, sniffling and drying my eyes with a piece of tissue. My nose and under my eyes were raw from the amount of times I had to wipe them.

Dominic rubbed his hand across his lips and chin and glared at me. His eyes read that he had been humiliated, and I didn't understand how or why. Finally, he spoke. "What the fuck was that shit you pulled back there?"

My face scrunched up in confusion because firstly, I didn't know what shit I had done, and two, I was grieving. He could have just asked me how I was feeling. Did I need rest? Something to eat? Something other than what the fuck he asked me.

"What shit did I pull?" I asked.

"All that hollering and dropping to the floor like you were a two-year-old? You are a grown-ass woman and you should handle yourself as such. That shit is unacceptable," he seethed.

"Excuse me?" I questioned. He had some fucking nerve.

"I said exactly what I said, and you heard me clearly."

"My mother just got lowered into the dirt and instead of consoling me, you're jumping down my throat because you thought that I should have reacted differently?"

"Like more of a woman than a toddler! Your ass is too big and heavy to be having to pick up off some damn ground 'cause you want to throw a temper tantrum!" Dominic yelled with spittle forming in the corners of his mouth.

"I – I – I'm what? What did you just say to me?" I was shocked. Granted, I've heard plenty of people make fun of my weight, but to hear it come from somebody that I loved did something slightly to my confidence. Dominic knew that he just fucked up. The look that covered his face said so.

"Babe, I'm sorry. I didn't mean that."

"Why would you say such a thing, Dominic?"

"I'm sorry. It was fucked up of me to say, and I admit that those words should not have come out of my mouth. You know I love every inch of your body."

What Dominic said was childish and I got what he meant. I adverted my eyes from Dominic's handsome face and looked out the window. For five minutes, he apologized and then he gave up. I sat silently with the wheels turning in my head. They didn't stop until I realized that we had reached his house instead of mine. I got out, slammed the door, and made my way to let myself in. I took my shoes off at the door and, I raced to the bar that was always fully stocked in the kitchen. I poured some whiskey in my cup, dropped two ice cubes inside, and raced upstairs to grab my suitcase.

"Mah'lani! What are you doing?" Dominic asked as he watched me move around the room like a crazy person.

"I was always told that if someone says something mean or hurtful and then apologizes and says they didn't mean to say it, they meant it. As soon as it slips through your lips, you meant every bit of it. I've heard hurtful things from people all my life and their opinion didn't matter. But as soon as you hear it from someone that you love, it becomes a different ball game," I explained as I swallowed my drink in one gulp.

"Babe, I'm truly sorry. I wasn't thinking at the moment and I can't see you walk out of that door. I slipped up and I just need you to forgive me," Dominic pleaded. He grabbed my hand and sat on the bed while I stood between his legs.

"I've already forgiven you," I said, touching the side of his face.

"Remember when I had left a couple of weeks ago and I accused you of leaving me?"

"You accused me of fucking other niggas, after you had just taken my virginity."

Dominic slightly rolled his eyes and began to speak again, "Anyway, the only reason why I reacted that way and accused you of those things is because I wouldn't know what I would do without you."

"But Dominic, you can't do that. You can't just say and do those things and think that things will just always be okay."

Dominic sighed and pinched the bridge of his nose. He said, "I'm not perfect. No one is. But I need to know if you will forgive me."

I looked down at him and everything in my body told me to not forgive him. That the way he was acting was red flags to something disastrous coming. But my dumb ass nodded my head and a smile formed on his face. Dominic stood up and kissed me like it would be his last kiss. My stomach growled, which stopped me from kissing him.

"How about we get changed and go get something to eat? I have been neglecting my body food for so long, I don't even know how I haven't passed out from starving myself," I suggested.

"I second that. I'm starving too."

We both got undressed and showered to have dinner at a seafood restaurant out in Albany. Things in that moment felt right. We laughed, joked, and drank like we were sailors out on the ocean. In my mind, I knew that this was how it was supposed to be, but something in my spirit told me to run.

Chapter Seven

See what y'all don't know about him
Is I can't let him go because he needs me
It ain't really him, it's stress from his job
And I ain't making it easy

February 14th is supposed to be the day for lovers. It was my first Valentine's Day with Dominic but as usual, when I had gotten home from work, he was nowhere to be found. I tried calling him, texting him, and I got nothing. I sat on the couch with a bottle of wine and watched chick flicks until I fell asleep. I'd been asleep for quite a few hours before I woke up when I heard his keys at the door. I sat up and searched for my bottle of wine. When he was fully inside, I threw the wine glass at him, missing him. It shattered against the wall next to him.

"What the fuck is your problem?" Dominic hissed. He stepped his tall frame into the living room and looked down at me sitting on the couch.

"Do you know what today is?" I asked, standing up from the couch.

"Any other day of the week. You must have lost your everlasting mind, throwing fucking glass at me."

"It's Valentine's Day, you fucking asshole. I cooked you dinner after working all day, thinking you would have the decency to come home on time and spend this night with me."

"Are you seriously giving me shit about a day? Who the fuck said I even celebrated this day? Who's to say that I celebrate anything other than my birthday?" Dominic spoke, giving me the stink face.

"That's not really the point here, Dominic. The point is that I have been talking to you about this for weeks now and you agreed that you would be here to spend it with me." I calmed my tone for a moment. I was upset, and I had let my anger to take over.

Dominic looked at me and walked towards me. We were face to face, damn near noses touching. His stare was intense, almost causing me to just give up, until I felt his hand around my neck and his grip getting tighter. This wasn't in a sexual way either. The tips of my toes were the only thing touching the floor and I struggled to breathe.

"Bitch, let me tell you one thing. You ever feel like you need to throw something at me, you better be ready for some repercussions. 'Cause one thing for sure and two things for certain: ain't no bitch of mine gonna disrespect me. Now you need to know that if you want me to do things, you need to go about it a different way. And what you going to do is fix me a damn plate, bring it to me upstairs, and take your silly drunk ass to bed. Do we have an understanding?" The fire in his eyes danced around with seriousness.

If I said anything other than to agree with him, then I knew things for sure wouldn't go well. Dominic let go of my neck and blood rushed to my brain as I gasped for air. I dropped to my knees and watched as he walked away. *What the fuck just happened?* I thought to myself. Dominic disappeared and I got up from the floor. The aroma from the food that I had cooked hours ago wafted in the air as I began to open pots and make Dominic his food. As it heated up in the microwave, I cleaned the kitchen, put the food away, and cleaned up the glass that I had thrown against the wall. I was still trying to figure out what had just happened.

When I made it to the room, Dominic was just getting out of the shower and had a towel around his waist. My mouth watered as his body dripped, and what he had just done to me was pushed to the back of my mind. Gathering myself, I placed his plate on the table on his side of the bed. As I turned away, he grabbed me by the arm and pulled me into him so that my face was buried into his chest. His strong arms wrapped around my body and I listened to his heartbeat thunder in my ear.

"Listen, ma, you can't be going around throwing shit at me. You have no idea how bad I wanted to murder you in just that instant. I love you, but there is just some shit that you can't do. There is shit that you may think is okay, but it will make me want to put you six feet under. I can't promise the next time I will hold anything back. I am the king of this castle and I will be treated as such." He brushed my hair away from my face and looked into my eyes.

I knew he was serious, but I didn't allow it to put fear in me. I let him go and proceeded to grab the laundry. Even at almost four in the morning, I did what I had to do to keep the house calm.

"How was the food?" I asked once I had put the laundry in the dryer. I picked up the plate to go wash it, but he stopped me by putting his hand on mine.

"Get in the bed. I'll take this down when I get up. It's almost five. You have to meet with Keana to clean out you and your mom's house."

I stopped myself from getting in the bed with one knee planted firmly on the mattress. I asked, "Now why would I do such a thing? And since when did it become okay for you to make decisions about what I am going to do with my mom's house with Keana?"

"Mah'lani, you are moving in with me. It doesn't make any sense for you to keep that house. It's just extra bills that we don't need. We gonna put it on the market, or even better, rent it out and collect the money. If you trust me, then just do what I say."

I got under the covers and pulled them up to my chin as my thoughts rambled around in my head. Why was he talking about what was good for me with Keana? Nobody knew what was good for me except me. My life felt like it was closing in on me and shit was changing. And I didn't like it one bit.

***

I woke up around eleven to Dominic bringing me breakfast in bed. I figured that it was his way of apologizing to me. When I was done eating, I jumped into the shower and quickly washed up so as to not keep Keana waiting. As I got dressed, Dominic walked into the room, took one look at me, and told me to change my clothes. Taken by surprise, I looked in the full-length mirror, wondering what the fuck I had on that would make him say that to me. I wore black tights under ripped-up jeans and a crème colored cashmere sweater that stopped just above my belly button. My jeans were high waisted so not much skin was showing, and I didn't think there was anything wrong with my outfit.

"What's wrong with what I am wearing?" I asked.

"You have skin showing."

"Barely. And that is an issue why?"

"Nobody wants to see that."

My forehead creased as I tried to figure out just what the fuck it was that he was trying to say to me. I asked, "Exactly who is going to see me that should be concerned with what I'm wearing? On my off days I always dress like this."

"Mah'lani, you should really start thinking about what it is that you wear on your days off. Girls your size shouldn't show excess skin."

"Excuse me?"

"I'm just saying that if you don't consider covering up some, you may be subjected to people saying mean things to you."

A chuckle escaped my mouth as I rolled my eyes and grabbed my bag to get ready to leave. I said, "In case you haven't noticed, I couldn't give a flying fuck as to what any motherfucker has to say about what I wear. I've heard it all my life, including from somebody I love. I couldn't care less about what somebody got to say about me now."

Dominic grabbed my arm and said, "Well I'm telling you to go change. You too damn big to be out here dressing like that."

My stomach knotted as I heard him clearly. The first time I let it slide, but I knew I heard what he said. I stared at him for a few moments longer and slowly walked away. Inside the bedroom, I changed into sweatpants and an oversized t-shirt, with my Ugg boots. Without another word, I walked out of the house and made it to mine in less than twenty minutes. Keana was already there but had gotten nowhere and she was browsing on her phone. With a hot cup of coffee from Dunkin Donuts in my hand, I took my shoes off and exhaled.

"How long have you been here?" I asked.

"Since almost eight. You were supposed to be here. What the hell happened?"

"With what?"

"Why is it almost one in the afternoon and you just now bringing your ass over this way?"

In my mind, I wanted to tell Keana what had happened, but Dominic and I had come to an agreement and it wouldn't happen again, so I didn't bring it up. "I didn't know this was happening, first of all. I did not agree to this. Beside that point, I didn't go to bed until sometime after five. It was a long night."

"What do you mean you didn't know anything about this?"

"Dominic didn't tell me he decided to sell my mom's house. He suggested that if I didn't want to sell, then I could just rent it out."

Keana sat up straight up on the couch and finally put her phone down. She said, "What the fuck do you mean he decided to sell your mama house? What did you say? I hope you said no, only because you didn't agree to it. The only reason why I'm here is because he said that it was your idea."

Tears dripped from my eyes. "I lost my mama not too long ago. Why would I get rid of this house?"

"That's the exact question that I wanted to know, but he kept saying that you wanted to do this."

"He wants me to move in with him and I'm fine with that, but what would I do with my mother's things? For sure I can't just throw it out. This was her life. Everything since I was a little girl."

"I know, love. I have memories too. If you are completely sure about moving in with Dominic, we could place your mom's things in storage and then go from there."

Sighing, I said, "I don't even want to think about that now. I just want a nice stiff drink and my bed."

Keana rose to her feet and held her hands out for me to grab. She said, "Come on, let's get this done. The faster we get it done, the sooner we can get wasted. It seems like since we became working, responsible adults we haven't been hanging out much. Plus, you got this man taking up all your time. Oh, and what happened to your neck?"

Instantly, my hand went to my neck as I felt the welts of Dominic's handprint from squeezing so hard. I looked at Keana and for the first time, I lied to my best friend. "Dominic and I got a little rough the other night and - "

"Nope! You know what? Forget that I asked," Keana responded and walked away. Although laughter was coming from my mouth, I really wanted to scream for help.

Keana and I had been packing and jamming for almost four hours straight and we had only gotten as far as the kitchen, living room, downstairs bathroom, and half of the guest bedroom down there. I took it upon myself to call it a night. Keana sat on the couch and placed a movie on the TV, since those were the only two items left in the living room, and poured us some drinks. Ten minutes into the movie, I checked my phone and there was a text message from Dominic letting me know that he had a few things to take care of and that he would be home late. Acknowledging that it was okay, I sent him a few heart eyes emojis and kissy faces, then put my phone away.

"Keana?" I said in a questioning tone.

"Yeah, babes? You need another refill?" she responded without taking her eyes off the TV. She had put on her favorite movie, *Sex in the City*, the first one.

"No. You know that Dominic and I have been together for almost seven months now, right?"

"Yes, why?"

"I know that he owns a few restaurants, but how he got them is what I don't know. You think if I ask Dominic he would tell me?"

Keana paused the movie and giggled. She looked at me and said, "So he could tell you what, exactly? The obvious?"

"What do you mean? The obvious?"

"You seriously don't know?"

The confusion etched on my face was apparent as I asked, "What do you know that I don't? Oh my God, please don't tell me that he out here selling and slinging dick."

"What!" Keana yelled and plugged her ears. She continued, "Why the fuck would you think that, of all things?"

There was an awkward pause between us before I asked her again what she knew. Keana claimed that she didn't want to tell me anything that Dominic didn't tell me and that this shit should be a conversation that I should have with him. She claimed that she didn't want to come in between two of her friends.

I snapped. "Bitch, I am your best friend. You just met that nigga, just like I did. So whatever you know, you better fucking spill the beans."

Keana rolled her eyes only because she knew that I was right. She folded her arms across her chest and looked at me like she was going to challenge me. I kept a straight face, letting her know that I wasn't going to back down. She huffed and puffed for a few moments and then she finally opened her mouth to speak. She said, "I heard it from Randy. Dominic is some type of kingpin, but only a few know of his status because he's low-key about it."

"A what? A fucking kingpin? How can I have been with him for these seven months and not know?" I was furious, to say the least. How could I not know?

"Girl, how could you not know? You've described his behavior to me and my thoughts automatically went to him being a drug dealer. It was either that or the nigga was cheating."

"Wait, you said that you heard it from Randy. I thought you been stopped fucking with him."

"I have zero niggas trying to knock this box down and rearrange my organs. He's the only one willing to do so, and from time to time, I let him. So what? But that's not what we are talking about currently," Keana sassed me.

I leaned back, trying to make sense of this because of his late nights, business trips, and middle of the night disappearances. Did I bring this up to him? Should I stay with him? I couldn't be involved with any raids or the police. I worked for the state, for God's sake. My mind was tripping me out and everything I had thought about.

"Look, Mah'lani, there is no reason for you to beat yourself up over this. I didn't want to tell you because I know how you get. You take things and make them into something bigger when it shouldn't be. Just take this information that you know and wait until he decides to tell you himself. If you not going to leave him over it, don't dwell on it."

"I just can't believe it."

"Don't dwell on it, Mah'lani. Are you going to go back to Dominic's tonight?"

"No, he said he was going to be staying out late. I'm gonna go sleep in my bedroom one last night."

"Okay, babes. If you need me, I'm only one phone call away."

I nodded with a smile on my face. Keana gathered her things and made her way to the door. Grabbing the bottle of 1800 coconut, I walked towards my room, stopping at my mother's room. Her room was left just the way it was. Her perfumes and lotions all sat neatly in formation on her dresser, her clothes were hung in color coordination in her closet, and her shoes were lined the same way.

"Mama, I wish you could be here. I need you so much. I don't know what to do. I feel so stressed out," I said out loud. I felt myself getting ready to bawl like a baby, so I closed the door and continued to my room.

Once there, I realized that I was more fucked up then I intended to be. The bottle of 1800 went on top of my dresser as I stripped out of my clothes and remained naked. Climbing into my bed, I looked at the time and saw that it was just after nine. With nothing to do, I forced myself to sleep.

***

Meanwhile…

At a dark oak table that sat twelve, twenty men were in the room clinging to every word that Dominic spoke. Twelve of the most important men on his team sat at the table while the rest of the men stood around. This was their monthly meeting and a celebration. It'd been six months and the operation had been free of police activity, and no one had been locked up or at war. Dominic ended the meeting by telling his men to stay safe. Everyone filed out of the room except for Dominic's right hand man, and a dude named Malcolm.

"Randy, thank you for always having my back. This is stressful shit, and too many times as I take this shit out on you, have you running around like a chicken with its head cut off, or even following me when I have dumb-ass ideas. I appreciate it nonetheless," Dominic spoke and reached his hand out for Randy to shake.

"You my brother from another mother. You've been there with me when I was at my lowest, and I will never forget that. It's only in my nature to have your back like you have mine," Randy responded. They shook hands and hugged each other.

"Now let's get down to business. Randy, can you go get Keana?"

Randy nodded his head and walked out of the room. Dominic looked at Malcolm. He was in his fifties, but easily could pass for his late thirties or early forties. Randy came back into the room with Keana and they joined Malcolm and Randy at the table.

"You know that if Mah'lani found out that I was here, she would kill me," Keana expressed while rolling her eyes.

"You are here for only one purpose, and it's for the sake of Mah'lani. You've known her longer than anyone of us in the room."

Keana rolled her eyes because she thought that this was a bad idea. Randy had told Keana of Dominic's plan and from that point, she hated it. Keana eyed Randy from where she sat. He was fine as shit to her and their relationship was much more than what she had made it to be to her best friend. Randy was more than just some dick. Randy thought the same and they both agreed to keep what they had private. Keana's gaze went to Malcolm and her eye rolling came back.

"You have some fucking nerve to show up to Mama Cheryl's funeral with your little family. Bad enough you've been gone for twenty-six years. Why would you want to come back now?" Keana questioned.

Malcolm coolly licked his lips and sat back in the high back leather chair. He thought over his words and began to speak, "There are things that kept me away that I would only care to discuss with Mah'lani."

"Before you get anywhere near my girl, you need to tell myself and her best friend everything so we not looking stupid finding shit out when she does," Dominic explained.

"You know that she's gonna be pissed with you, Dominic. This nigga been down with your organization for the past four years. She looks exactly like this nigga. As soon as you found out about her being fatherless, you should have put two and two together."

"Randy, get your girl."

"Randy ain't gonna do shit. To protect her, you should have said something. You claim you love her, but you are keeping secrets. You ain't no better than this nigga sitting here."

"And you are? Are you not keeping a secret from her by being here? Did you not hide the fact that you knew her mother was ill and dying? You are no better than me with keeping secrets, Keana." Dominic was annoyed with Keana. She acted like she was better than him, and that was something he didn't like because he felt like women should stay in their place. She was lucky that he was best friends with his girl or she wouldn't be here at all.

"You're hiding the fact that you're a kingpin, like that isn't a crime. My girl may not be street, but my nigga, my ears stay to them and you need to tell her before I do."

Randy decided that enough was enough. Here these two were spreading business in front of someone whose identity they just found out. Randy spoke calmly. "Listen, y'all both have Mah'lani's interest at best here. Whatever beef y'all got going on, y'all need to squash that shit."

Keana sucked her teeth and yet again rolled her eyes. She was beginning to get a bad taste in her mouth about Dominic, but Randy was right. They were there on behalf of Mah'lani, so she would put Dominic's behavior to the back of her mind.

"Okay, Malcolm. Spill the beans and let us know why you were gone for so long." Keana sighed, over the situation already.

Malcolm folded his hands in front of him and began to talk. He said, "When Cheryl told me that she was pregnant with Mah'lani, I was involved in some things that were going to send me to jail. I didn't punk out so as to not take care of my responsibilities, but I didn't want Cheryl to bring a child into this world when I wouldn't be able to be around to take care of her. To be able to witness her birth, first time crawling, her first word, her first everything… I also didn't want Cheryl

82

to worry about my illegal activity, so I told her that I was married. Two months after Cheryl told me she was pregnant, I was shipped to prison. I thought she had gotten an abortion, to be quite honest, but several months later, my mother came to visit me, and she told me that Cheryl had showed up with a newly born Mah'lani, telling her that this was my child.

"My mother told her where I was. Told her that I lied about being married. She told her that I had lied to protect my unborn child. Cheryl was my everything. I loved her tremendously and at the time, I thought that I was doing the right thing. In hindsight, I should have showed more compassion, because my only child grew up fatherless anyway."

Keana interrupted and asked, "Wait, so those kids that you showed up with at the funeral weren't yours?"

"Hell no. I just got out of jail five years ago. The woman I was with, I met her not long after I had gotten out. I'm not even playing daddy to those disrespectful heathens. When I found out that Cheryl passed, she nagged me until my ears bled for her to tag along."

"So why now? Why do you want to show up in Mah'lani's life? Don't you think this would be too much for her?" That was Dominic.

"Of course, I think so. Her mama is gone, the only parent that she knew, but I want to make up for those missing years. Even if she's not receptive, I want to at least try to my last dying breath to do so."

The room was still, and thunder rolled. Everyone in the room had their own thoughts to process. Keana didn't know whether to take him serious or not. Mah'lani, her best friend – no, her sister - had been through a great deal, and all she wanted to do was make sure that her best friend was happy again.

"Mah'lani's birthday is in a few weeks. I'm throwing her a surprise birthday party. I will give you the details. If you are serious about this, you will show up. If not, I will pay and never come back again. Do we have an understanding?" Dominic asked in a serious tone.

"We do. But you can keep your money in your pocket. I'm serious about this," Malcolm stated.

With that, everyone gave each other a look that said they hoped that Mah'lani would accept this.

Chapter Eight

To show just how much we love you
And I'm sure you would agree
It couldn't fit more perfectly
Than to have a world party
On the day you came to be

"Happy birthday, beautiful," Dominic said. He was leaning over me with a tray of food and a smile as wide as the Grand Canyon.

There were eggs with cheese, sausages, bacon, homemade fries with peppers and onions, toast, and some coffee. It was five o' clock in the morning, an hour before I actually had to get up for work. The gesture was nice, but it felt like I had just fallen asleep. Dominic decided the night before to have his way with me, no matter how tired I was. In his words, he wanted to give me birthday sex.

I allowed him to place the tray of food over my legs and kissed him and thanked him. For it to be so early, he was in a damn good mood, like it was his birthday.

"You're in a good mood," I mentioned, shoveling eggs into my mouth and sipping the coffee.

"I'm just happy to be celebrating your birthday with you. This is the first of many to come."

"That's right."

"Quick question. We've never really spoken about having kids. Of course, it's too soon now, but eventually, I would like to have a little Dominic and little Mah'lani running around here. Firstly, we would have to get you into the gym to lose a few pounds so that we could make sure that you and the baby are healthy."

I stopped eating my food because what he said disgusted me. I let it slide though because it was my birthday and I didn't want it to be shitty.

"Dominic, I hate to upset you, but I can't have children," I calmly said.

"How can you not if you've only had sex with me?" he asked, confused.

"When I was a teenager, I was having trouble with my periods. They were irregular. My mom took me to several doctors and they've all said the same thing. My fallopian tubes were damaged at age seventeen, so they took out both of my tubes. I will not ever be able to have children."

Dominic became quiet as he searched his mind to say something. The look on his face said that he was trying to understand what I had just said. In a slow, steady tone, Dominic asked, "Your uterus and ovaries are good though, right? Because if that's in working order, you should be able to have children."

I sighed because I hated to have this conversation. People who didn't understand pelvic inflammatory disease always assume that if my uterus and ovaries work, it was still easy for me to get pregnant. And that is not the case. There is a one percent chance that I could get pregnant, so I just accepted the fact that I would not be able to have children.

"There is a one percent chance that I can. There is also the option of IVF, but I've already accepted the fact that I won't be having any." Moving the covers off me, I got out of the bed and continued, "Can we talk about this another time? It's my birthday and I don't want to be sad. I promise we could talk about this in the future when you decide the time is right. Hell, even tomorrow. Just let me enjoy my birthday today."

Dominic stood up and took my hands in his. He spoke softly, "You're right. Today is your special day. I want to take you out after work so come straight home, get all sexy, and the night will be yours."

A smile crept onto my face as I kissed his lips. I sat on the bed to finish enjoying my breakfast, but Dominic had other plans. He pushed me down onto the bed and spread my legs wide open. He used his index fingers in between my womanly folds. My love juices leaked onto his fingers as chills went up and down my spine. His tongue replaced his fingers as it flicked over my clit, causing it to thump. My moans and his tongue lapping away at my goodness were the only noises in the room.

"Please...don't.... stop," I moaned.

"Tell me you love me," he murmured against my pussy.

My back arched, and my fingers grabbed ahold of the sheets as little black dots danced in front of my eyes.

"Oh God! I love you, Dominic!"

The way my body reacted to him was mind-blowing. Five minutes hadn't even gone by and I was ready to splash my juices all over his face. Dominic stood from between my legs as his face dripped with my wetness. I was about to get up, but Dominic placed his hand on my shoulder and began to stroke himself as he slid his fingers between my slit. Dominic's fingers worked their magic as he brought me to climax again and this time he came with me, spraying his nut all over my stomach and vagina. I wanted to go to sleep, but I knew that I had to get ready for work. Rolling out of the bed and heading to the shower, that is exactly what I did.

***

Work had drained me. Clarissa took me out in the field to do home visits. On one case we had to call the cops to be involved because the parents wouldn't allow us access to checking on the kids. The mother was an obnoxious piece of shit who was not only acting bossy to us, but her husband as well. I felt bad for the guy because he looked like he was stuck in a bad hypnotic movie. He walked around in sort of a trance-like state and it was all bad. To make matters worse, I didn't get off until close to seven because of a ton of paperwork that I didn't want to do the next day.

When I arrived home, I saw that Dominic had left me a note to automatically get ready and that he would be home shortly after to pick me up and whisk me away to dinner. I rushed into the bathroom and quickly showered, leaving my clothes all over the floor. After climbing out of the tub, I wrapped a towel around my body, quickly picked my clothes up, and threw them in the hamper. I grabbed my coconut and shea body butter and sat on the bed to moisture my skin. On the bed was a black garment bag that I hadn't noticed before. After using the body butter, I cleaned my hands off and opened the bag. There was a red halter dress, made by Vera Wang, in the garment bag. The dress was so soft to the touch, I thought it was going to melt in my hands. The dress came down to my feet, had slits on the sides, right near the boob area, and a slit down the back. The straps came close to my neck. There was also a pair of shiny, crystal-encrusted Louboutin red bottom silver strappy shoes.

As I quickly got dressed my phone dinged, letting me know a text message had come in. I ran to my phone. Dominic had texted, saying that he was going to be waiting outside for me. I let him know that all I had to do was fix my hair and apply a bit of makeup, and I would be out. Cursing, I swooped my hair into a bun at the nape of my neck, placed my diamond necklace on my neck and the matching earrings in my ears. I opted out of the makeup and threw on simple lip gloss. Racing to the closet, I searched to find a matching coat to go along with my dress. My mouth dropped when I saw the snow-white waist-length mink coat hanging up. Dominic had gone all out with my outfit and I couldn't wait to show him how much I appreciated it. Taking just my phone and lip gloss, I rushed out of the house and through the doors, pausing as I saw my tall, fine, delicious-looking man leaning against a black stretch limo with a bouquet of red roses. A smile crept onto my face as I slowly walked up to him. He was dressed in a white suit, red silk shirt, white bowtie, and red loafers. His bald head glistened under the street light.

"You look fucking beautiful," he whispered to me as he brushed a strand of hair out of my face that had fallen loose.

"And you, sir, just take my breath away," I spoke, looking directly into his eyes. At that moment, all the sly shit he was saying about my weight went out of the window. I chalked it up to him just stressing and figured he really didn't mean it. He wouldn't buy me such revealing outfits if he did.

"Are you ready to have a fun night?"

"Of course. It's been a while since I let my hair down."

Dominic laughed, handed me my flowers, and opened the door for me. I climbed in and got comfortable with the ride. We ended up at Mallozzi's Banquet and Ballroom in Rotterdam. On the way, Dominic let me know we were gonna grab something to eat and go out to have drinks and to dance the night away.

When we entered the building, there was a room that was dark, and a host was standing at a podium. Dominic walked over to the guy and whispered something to him. The guy nodded and told us to follow him. We began to walk to the dark room. When he clicked on the light, I saw that there was a small table adorned with some more red roses. A smile formed on my face as we went further into the room. The host handed us menus as we sat down at the table.

"Dominic, where are the people? Shouldn't there be other diners in here?" I asked.

There were flowers adorning each corner of the massive room. A banner over the door said "Happy birthday, Mah'lani" and balloons were placed sporadically around the room.

"Sure, but I rented the place for a night to make sure that the most beautiful woman in the world has a wonderful birthday," he responded.

Just as I was going to say thank you, the lights turned off and my heart leaped to get up from the table, but Dominic held my hand, comforting me, letting me know that I was in good hands. A light flickering on the wall caught my attention. Dominic made his way to me and asked me to stand up.

"Dominic, what's going on?" I asked nervously.

"Shhh," was his simple response.

The light stopped flickering and a slideshow began to play from a projector hidden inside of the room. Dominic stood behind me and wrapped his arms around my waist as we watched pictures throughout my life being displayed on the wall. "Superwoman" by Alicia Keys played and as each picture went by, I cried. Pictures that I had not seen in years were on display. Seeing my mom again in those old pictures did something to my heart. Alicia Keys ended, and my mother's voice played loud and clear as she read "Phenomenal Woman" by Maya Angelou. There was a still picture of me the day I had graduated college and my mom reciting that poem was back from when I graduated high school. She had read the poem to me in such a powerful voice I had felt it was Maya Angelou reciting it to me herself. Keana had recorded it, and I could kill her at this moment. Once the poem was finished, I knew my makeup would have been too, if I had worn some. The lights hadn't come on yet, but I turned around to place a thousand kisses on Dominic while crying my thanks to him. Finally, the lights came on and behind Dominic were our close friends, my coworkers, and of course Keana, yelling out, "Surprise!"

I looked up at Dominic. There was a smile on his face. To say I was surprised was an understatement. Everybody whooped and hollered as more tears cascaded down my face. Keana came running to me and hugged me tight.

"I hate you so much right now," I whispered in her ear.

"Don't hate me. This was your man's idea." She giggled.

The party began as waiters and waitresses brought out extra chairs and tables, the DJ began to play music, and the open bar began to serve drinks. Looking around the room brought a smile to my face. The majority of the people that were there were Dominic's people, but it still warmed my heart that whether they knew me or not, they took time out of their day to spend my birthday with me.

Plenty of pictures were taken and I met some of the people that were closer to Dominic. Slowly but surely, he was letting me into his world. From across the room, I spotted Dominic with a drink in his hand eyeing me. I smiled and finger waved at him. He winked at me, raised his glass, and smiled. I was happier than a crackhead who saw a sign that said "free crack".

Two hours later, the music stopped and someone tapped on a microphone. It was Dominic, showing all his teeth as the room grew quiet. Keana was standing next to me, holding my hand as we averted our eyes to Dominic.

"First of all, I would like to thank everyone for coming out tonight to celebrate my baby's twenty-seventh birthday. It means a lot to both of us. I also want to mention that it has begun to snow, and I'd like for everyone to be safe when leaving here tonight," Dominic stated.

"It's already the middle of March. I'm tired of this damn snow!" someone shouted from behind me, causing the room to erupt in laughter.

Once the room settled down, Dominic continued to talk.

"I wanted this day to be special for my future wife because not too long ago, she lost her mother due to cancer. I admired her relationship with her mother because they were so close and there was nothing that I could have done to be able to fill that void in her heart. Seeing this woman broken did something to me and my hand to God, I will for as long as I walk this earth make sure that I make her the happiest woman alive." Dominic paused for a dramatic effect, taking in all of the "aw's" and screeching from the women in the room. What he said sounded good to everybody else, but I couldn't help but slightly cringe and roll my eyes. Flashbacks of him choking me and his spiteful words reminded me of the two different personalities he possessed.

"Baby, come up here really quick," Dominic said through the mic.

With a smile on my face, I sashayed, with a natural sway in my hips, up to my man with a smile on my face.

"What's up?" I asked, looking deeply in his eyes.

Then it hit me that he was saying all these good things because he was about to propose. Isn't that what people do before they drop to their knee and ask the love of their life to marry them? My eyes darted to Keana, who was patting her eyes dry and I knew then that she was in on this too. Was I ready for this? Being married to someone I barely knew? People do that all the time right?

"I want you to meet somebody."

I looked at him with confusion written on my face. I was relieved that he wasn't proposing, but confused nonetheless. I asked, "Who?"

"Malcolm, where you at?" Dominic spoke loudly.

I peered into the crowd. I saw the guy from my mom's burial holding a bouquet of long-stemmed sunflowers. He stood in front of me and nervously handed me the flowers.

"Dominic, who is this?" I whispered away from the mic.

"Malcolm, finally you get to meet your daughter. Mah'lani, babe, this is your dad," Dominic said into the microphone, which I wish he hadn't done. The crowd erupted in thunders of applause and females were patting their eyes.

"My what!" I screeched.

Dominic quickly darted his eyes at me, signaling to me to hold my tongue. Beyoncé's "Daddy" began to play and this man, who was supposedly my father, took my hands and began to dance with me.

"Happy birthday," he simply said.

People were taking pictures, so I was forced to have a smile on my face like this was the happiest moment of my life.

"I cannot believe this bullshit," I said more to myself. I found myself laughing like a crazy person as Beyoncé sang about how she wanted her unborn son to be like her daddy. I couldn't relate to that shit with a ten-foot pole. If any son of mine I had or adopted turned out like this fool who was my father, I was throwing the whole child away. No way in hell would I raise someone to abandon their child, under any circumstances.

"I can explain everything," Malcolm said.

"You don't have to, 'cause I don't give a shit. Dominic forced me into this and at this point, both of you niggas can kiss my ass." I just wanted this song to be over so I could take a few minutes to myself. All of this was too much for me and what was supposed to be an amazing day for me had quickly turned to a shit show.

Keana was off in the corner talking to Dominic and her eyes met mine. She mouthed "sorry" to me and I rolled my eyes. She knew somebody had fucked up, and I'm sure that my mother was slowly rolling over in her grave.

Beyoncé was finally done singing and I tried to walk away. Malcom looked at me with a pleading look. Malcolm held onto my hand and Dominic walked over again with that stupid-ass microphone.

"I didn't plan on doing this today, but I guess today would be the perfect time to do it. Mah'lani, you already know that I've planned on spending the rest of my life with you. Since the moment I met you, seeing you for the first time, I automatically knew it was love at first sight. Malcolm, I would like it if you gave me the permission to make Mah'lani my wife."

"How the fuck you gonna ask him and he hasn't been in my life at all?" I asked Dominic, who must have slipped on some ice or something.

Dominic now had an embarrassed look on his face. Malcolm's eyes fell to the floor and Keana's mouth hung open. Everyone looked on in confusion.

"Not now, Mah'lani," Dominic seethed through his teeth while placing a smile on his face.

"Then when?" I asked.

Dominic handed the microphone to Malcolm and back to me again. Malcolm placed the microphone to his lips and said, "Dominic, yes you could. I know that you are a good dude and I couldn't imagine another dude making her his wife."

My mouth dropped, and I knew this was a fucking joke. Why did he feel like he could give anyone permission? For the last time, I sucked it up, placed a smile on my face and looked down at Dominic, who was on his knee with a gorgeous vintage floral halo diamond ring set in white gold.

"Will you do the honor of being my wife?" Dominic asked.

I was too pissed to say yes, so I just settled on nodding my head and fake crying. Forced tears slid down my face as Dominic placed the ring on my finger. Dominic stood up and wrapped his arms around my waist and his lips on mine. Applause erupted.

"I'm going to the bathroom," I told Dominic and excused myself. I grabbed Keana by the hand and dragged her with me. Once inside the bathroom, I paced back and forth, trying to calm myself because the level of my pisstivity was through the roof.

"This was all Dominic's idea," Keana began. She continued, "I told him this wasn't a good idea, but he insisted that your father make an appearance."

"That man is not my father!" I yelled with my hands on my hips.

"Mah'lani, I know that you are mad, but - "

"Mad? Mad! Keana, mad went out of the window when he invited this nigga to give me to him. That man has not been in my life, not even for one second, and to give him that much power is ridiculous."

"He has a reason as to why he wasn't there, Mah'lani. And I think you should give him a chance and hear him out."

"What? Keana, do you hear what you said? He ran like a bitch-ass nigga from his responsibilities, and now he wants to make things right? He was at my mama's burial and didn't even say two words about it. Just flaunting his wife and two bastard-ass kids."

"That's not his wife or kids," Keana mumbled under her breath.

I looked at her with a questioning look because she sure knew a whole lot. I said, "You sure do know a lot for all this to be on Dominic. Yet again, you are withholding important information from me."

"It ain't got nothing to do with me withholding anything from you. This is a conversation you need to have with your father."

"He is not my father!" I yelled yet again.

Keana threw her hands up in surrender. She gazed at me for a moment and turned to walk away. I looked at myself in the mirror, and my eyes were puffy and red. Grabbing some tissue from the stall, I patted under my eyes and tried to make myself look a little more presentable. The glistening from my ring caught my attention as I was making sure that my hair was intact. A voice in my head told me to put on my big girl panties and ride this wave. The party should be coming to an end soon and people were going to have to answer my questions tonight or I would pack my things and disappear. Taking a deep breath, I closed my eyes to catch my bearings and then opened them.

"You okay?" Dominic's voiced echoed in the empty bathroom. I hadn't noticed that he had entered the bathroom.

"Yes, I'm okay. There was too much in such little time that was going on for me to process. I just needed to gather myself," I responded with a slight smile on my face.

"Are you sure? I could tell that you were a bit thrown off with your father showing up."

"We can talk about it later. There are people waiting. For the record, he is not my father," I spoke, the smile now gone from my face.

Dominic gave me a look as I walked away from him and out of the bathroom. He wanted to throw a party for my enjoyment, and that is exactly what was going to happen.

I avoided Malcolm for the most part and got drunk so that I could forget about everything that had happened, even if it was momentarily.

***

By midnight, the party had wrapped up and I was drunk off my ass. After we had finished cleaning the ballroom, Dominic, Keana, Randy, Malcolm, and myself walked to the limo to head on over to mine and Dominic's massive house. As they talked among themselves, I drowned them out. The only one that I was not currently beefing with was Randy. I'm sure that he knew about all of this, but he had yet to say anything about what was going on.

Everyone climbed out of the limo once we arrived with Dominic leading the way. Keana pushed her way through the guys and wrapped her arm through mine, providing me with unspeakable comfort.

"Everybody can have a seat in the living room while I pour us a round. Mah'lani, you need some water to sober up some," Dominic instructed.

Rolling my eyes, I sat in the single seat because I refused to allow any of these betrayers to sit next to me.

"Mah'lani!" Malcolm called my name.

My eyes averted to him in a what-the-fuck-you-want manner.

"What's up?" I asked.

"I'm sorry to just impose on you like this, but I have to let you know why I wasn't there. I feel like I owe you that much."

A gut-wrenching laugh attempted to escape my lips, but I only managed to pass it off as a chuckle. Dominic showed up with a Corona for everyone and bottled water for me. I accepted it and said, "What makes you think that I would remotely care about why you weren't in my life? It's been twenty-seven years. Don't you think that it's just a tad bit too late?"

"To be honest with you, I would feel the exact same way that you do. My dad died when I was just seven years old. He was my everything. He'd take me to the movies, sporting events, the circus, you name it, and we were there. When he died, a piece of me died as well. I went through life wishing that he was by my side every step of the way. I have spent so much time away from you for selfish reasons and I just want to make it up to you," Malcolm stated.

"Selfish reasons, huh? I couldn't care less about any of the reason as to why you haven't been there. I've made it this far without you, and I'm pretty sure that I can continue to do so."

The room was silent as Malcolm looked around at everyone. Dominic tapped me on my shoulder and gestured for me to follow him. Excusing ourselves, I followed Dominic upstairs and into our bedroom. He closed the door behind us once we were inside of the room. Reaching behind my back, I reached for my zipper and let the dress fall from my body. Dominic grabbed me by the arm and slammed me against the wall, my head banging against it from the impact.

"What the hell is wrong with you?" Dominic seethed.

"I don't particularly care what the fuck that nigga has to say. I don't give a fuck where he was at. I don't even give a fuck that he is still breathing. He should have just died wherever he has been at for all these years."

"I am doing you a favor and you just want to fuck it all up. Your mom is dead and you have only myself and Keana. God forbid something happens to either of us, who are you going to have?"

"I know my mother is gone. You don't have to remind me."

"Hear the man out. I swear if you don't, so help me God, you will pay for it."

The look in Dominic's eyes burned a fire that I had never seen before. A fire that struck fear in me.

"Can I get into some comfortable pajamas?"

"When you are done, bring your fat ass downstairs so we can get this done and over with."

No apology. No eye contact. Nothing. I stood there with my mouth open as I put it together that no matter how many times he'd let that insult slip through his lips, he meant it every single time. Grabbing my super soft pajamas from the dresser, I changed and went back downstairs to listen to what Malcolm had to say – at least, I honestly tried to, but the word "fat" just kept ringing throughout my head. The night just needed to end already.

My mind was made up. There was no way in hell that I was going to make amends with Malcolm. He chose the way that he wanted his relationship with me would go, and that is something that he had to deal with.

Mimi

Chapter Nine

Making those promises that I could not keep
In my dark times, baby, this is all I could be
Only my mother could love me for me

Things between Dominic and I went from sugar to shit within five minutes, and it all began the day of my birthday three weeks ago. I heard Malcom out, but had not accepted him or returned any of his phone calls. When I said that I didn't want to deal with it, I meant it. My life had been reduced to going to work and coming home because I had little desire to do anything other than sit in the house with my cases to review and prepare for the next day. Hell, I'd barely seen Keana and I was glad I didn't. Dominic would often come home and take his anger out on me. Most times he would just scream and yell, call me out my name, or he would completely ignore me. Other times, times that he would come home drunk, was when he put his hands on me. Even knowing that this was wrong, I stayed with him. I stayed with him in hopes of things getting better.

The weather had finally broken and it was starting to feel like the springtime. Clarissa had stopped by the house Friday night, yesterday, for me to review and determine if the cases would go unfounded. Dominic was out handling whatever it was he had to, so with a bottle of wine and *How to Get Away with Murder* on the screen, I curled up on the couch and opened the first manila envelope. It was a case of a family of six: mom, dad, and four children. All boys. Dad was abusing mom and boys; the school had noticed bruises on the middle child and decided to get us involved. Clarissa and I made the home visit and noticed immediately that the father was abusive, manipulative, and controlling. He wouldn't allow the children or the mom to talk to us. We advised the mom to go to the courts, get an order of protection, and remove the dad from the household.

Going over the notes that were placed in the file, I found that the mom filed the protection order against the dad the next day after our arrival. The cops had come to remove the dad from the premises and it had been a month since he left. Mom has moved to a different location that was unknown to dad. There were scheduled supervised visits in our office every two weeks up until the dad showed some progress and attended anger management classes as well as fatherhood classes. Everything in the file told me that the kids were now in a safe environment and after one last home visit, I decided to note that the case could get closed. Three cups of wine later, I was done making all my notes and ready to take a break. And just as the thought passed through my mind, the doorbell rang throughout the house.

At the door, from what I could see through the glass partition, was an older woman and she was dressed pretty fancy in a purple pantsuit. By her side sat an object that stopped just an inch shy from her under boob. Confusion was displayed on my face when I opened the door and noticed there was a stroller with a child in it, possibly between one and two years of age. Beautiful girl too. My attention went to the woman, whom you could tell was an older woman, but you couldn't tell how much older. She could have been forty or as old as seventy and you wouldn't know, because black don't crack.

"Can I help you?" I asked the woman, who had eyes blocked by an oversized pair of Dolce and Gabbana shades.

Her head turned in my direction and she took the shades from her face. She revealed the lightest, most beautiful honey-colored, almond-shaped eyes I had ever seen.

"I'm looking for Dominic. Is he here?" she asked.

"No, he is not. I can tell him that you stopped by and have him give you a call. If you could hold on for a moment, I could run and grab a pen and paper, take your number down," I spoke as I began to walk away from the door.

"You don't need to do that," the woman called after me, stopping me in my stride.

"Can I at least get your name so that I can tell him that you dropped by?"

The woman looked at me up and down, making me feel uncomfortable, and then asked, "Are you his girlfriend?"

Holding my hand up, I smiled slightly and responded, "His fiancée."

"Oh. So he has decided to settle down and put a ring on someone's finger."

"Ma'am, who are you again?" I asked, trying to be as polite as I could be. She sure knew a lot about Dominic, but had yet to tell me who she was. The child in the stroller began to fidget in the stroller and fuss a tad bit.

"Do you mind if I come in to change my granddaughter? We drove from Atlanta and the last time I was able to check her diaper was when we were in Pennsylvania," the woman asked.

I wasn't going to tell this woman no. The toddler needed to be comfortable.

"Yes, sure," I responded quickly, allowing the woman who knew my fiancé to come inside. I leaned against the living room door frame and waited for her to finish.

"You know, when Dominic was growing up, I knew that he was going to make something of himself. I knew that he would take care of his family as soon as he made enough money. But I didn't expect for him to banish his own mother and child."

What the fuck is this lady talking about? I thought. He didn't have any kids, and his mother died.

"Um, what do you mean? He told me that he didn't have any children and that his mother passed two years ago."

"My child has always been a good liar. Clearly, I am not dead and that child lying on the couch is his. Now his child's mother died while giving birth to her. After she died and D'sani was able to come home from the hospital, Dominic left Atlanta and forced me to take care of her by myself. Of course, he has sent me money to help take care of her, but I am only getting older and so is D'sani. I cannot go around chasing her anymore. My arthritis is getting bad and I'd like to go and live the rest of my days the best that I can. It's time for Dominic to step up and do what it is that he is supposed to be doing. Not me."

I was in utter shock at what Dominic's mother had just spilled on me. My mouth went dry as it hung open and I was rendered speechless. Dominic was slowly unraveling and becoming someone that I didn't know. Dominic's mother started to walk around the living room, looking around at the art and numerous pictures that hung on the walls.

"Would you like for me to call him to come home?" It was the only thing that I seemed to think of to say.

"No. not yet. What else has he told you?"

"That's it."

"I'm Gloria, by the way. I'm surprised that he's settling down. And with a girl like you, no less."

"What do you mean with a girl like me?" I questioned. What could she possibly mean by that?

"He usually likes dumb girls, but you seem to be very smart. You are also someone who he, physically, isn't attracted to. You are a pretty woman, you just have a little more meat on your bones." Gloria looked me up and down.

"Oooh, you one of those people. Just because I'm a BBW, I can't have a fine dude like your son be interested with me?"

"That is not what I'm trying to say. I'm saying that you aren't his type. You can easily be another man's type, but I know my son. And I'm not entirely too sure what it is, but I know that you are just a project for him."

Keeping my cool, I folded my arms across my chest and said, "I don't know who you think you are talking to me the way that you are, but I've been nothing but polite with you, and right about now, you are pushing it. I don't care who you are. In my house, you fucking show some respect."

"Your house? This is my son's house!" Gloria raised her head in the air with her nose to the sky.

"You want to bet?" I asked with my eyebrow raised. I walked to my side table and opened the drawer. Grabbing the manila envelope that was in there, I passed it to Gloria and watched her open it and read the papers that were in there. When Dominic wanted me to sell my mother's house and move in with him, I told him that I would do so once he agreed to put my name on the deed, and he did.

"Why would he do something so ridiculous?"

"Because, despite what you think, he loves me. Period. Now, you can go if you can't act like a civilized person."

Gloria looked at me for a few moments and moved toward D'sani and began to gather her things.

"You can leave her. I'll make sure that he does what he is supposed to do," I spoke. There was no way that he was going to get away with not being a father, especially if he was talking about starting a family with me.

"I don't know you. I will not leave my grandchild with you."

"I am a social worker. I protect kids, not hurt them. Now grab your things and get the hell out of my house."

Gloria eyed me and grabbed her purse from the couch. When she got to the door, she turned to face me and said, "I will be taking Dominic to court."

I couldn't help but laugh and say, "You just made this whole speech about not wanting to worry about taking care of a child. And you told it to a social worker, no less. Get out now."

With anger written all over her face, Gloria twisted the doorknob and flung the door open, moving as fast as she could go. The slam of the door banging shut shocked little D'sani from her nap into a crying fit.

***

It was midnight. It took me the past three hours to calm D'sani down and put her to sleep. After her angry grandmother left, she cried for an hour until I was able to calm her down. I got D'sani to eat and get ready for bed was all good until I took her up to the guest bedroom to go to sleep. She screamed until her voice was hoarse and I had a headache. A glass of wine was needed as soon as I shut the door to the room. As I drank the wine, I cleaned up the mess that D'sani and I had made.

Headlights splashed across the windows and I knew that Dominic was home. It was about to be a long night.

Knowing that he was going to be hungry, I popped his food into the microwave and waited for him to make his entrance. When he did, he wore stress on his face, and just for a second, I thought about not saying anything about his daughter until the morning. I then thought about her waking up in the middle of the night in a crying a fit.

He kissed my cheek and said, "And how was your day today?"

"Long. Eventful. Informative, to say the least."

"Why so?"

Taking his food from the microwave I placed it on the counter. I spoke, "My day was planned out lovely. I was going to catch up with my cases, drink some wine, and possibly go out with Keana for dinner. But none of that happened at all."

"Yet again, I ask why not?"

"Can I ask you a question?"

"Sure," he said with food in his mouth.

"I get that your parents weren't the best growing up, but you have to understand that, for me, knowing your background and childhood means a lot to me. You put this ring on my finger and asked for me to move forward and begin planning the wedding."

Dominic stopped eating his food. He turned around and leaned against the counter, dusting his hands against his pants. Exhaling, he said, "I can't tell you much about my father, because he legit was never around. I knew who he was but when I'd see him on the streets, I would walk right past him. Before I was born, or even conceived, for that matter, my mom and dad were the best of friends. My dad started doing drugs once she became pregnant with me. She left him. He reappeared once I was born and resented my mother for leaving him and decided to trick her into doing drugs. She barely took care of me and I would always be at a different relative's house. When I was five, my mother died from an overdose and my aunt gained custody of me until I was about eleven. That's when I started hanging around the wrong people and began getting into a bunch of fights and mu aunt decided to place me into foster care. End of story."

My heart beat in my chest as I looked him directly in his eyes as he lied to me so effortlessly. His eyes never left mine as he lied directly to my face.

"The fact that you can sit here and lie to me in my face and lie to me so effortlessly amazes me," I said once he was done. The tears threatened to spill, but I willed them not to. First he said she died two years ago, and now he was telling me that she died when he was five.

"What do you mean? Lie to your face? Don't tell me that you are on your bullshit again. Tonight, I can't take this shit. I've had a stressful day and I would love to just eat and go to bed. Going back and forth with you about my life is not an option."

"There was a visitor today, Dominic. A ghost, actually."

Dominic looked on with a raised brow. Dominic sucked his teeth as if he was growing impatient with me. Dominic then laughed and spoke, "Yeah, you on some bullshit tonight because you are speaking in riddles. Have you been drinking?"

"I'm not playing these games with you anymore! I don't know why you feel the need to lie to me when I have done nothing bit told you my truth! You lied to me about your trip, said that you had to go to Memphis and then switched it to St. Louis. You told me that your mom died from an overdose when you were five but when I asked a while back, you said that she died two years ago. The only thing that was consistent with your story is that your father never was around! Oh, and how about when I asked you if you had any children and you told me no!"

Slap!

My neck snapped to the side so fast that I thought I had whiplash. Dominic stood over me with a scowl on his face, jaw twitching.

"You always think that you know something, when in fact you know nothing. You make up your own accusations and expect me to give you answers that I just don't have!"

"You don't know how to deal with pressure, so you put your hands on me? I should have never continued this thing that you want to call a relationship. You have lied to me and have lowered my self-esteem to the point that I don't know whether I'm coming or going. You claim that you love me, but you don't fucking show it!" I yelled. I was through with whatever that this was we had going on. For a few more seconds I looked at Dominic and decided that this was it. I was leaving. I climbed up the stairs and once inside the room, I threw my things around the room, looking for suitcases, and duffel bags.

"Where do you think you are going? You don't get to accuse me of things and leave."

"I do what I want to do! I'm not accusing you of anything, Dominic! Just leave me alone!" Finding the suitcase, I opened it and began to throw my belongings inside.

Dominic grabbed me by the arm and jerked me so hard that I spun away from him and landed into the wall with a thud. He followed up by putting his hand around my throat and squeezed it.

"You don't get to leave me," Dominic seethed. He swung me once again, and I landed face down on the bed with Dominic straddling my waist and twisting my arm against my back.

"Get off of me, Dominic." I panicked because I just knew that he was going to break my arm.

The blow shocked me and then took the breath out of me. Dominic had sucker punched me in my side, a kidney shot. He pulled my hair and slammed my head into the bed, probably wishing that it was the floor. He would not let me go and his heavy frame held me down in place, making it hard for me to breathe.

"You are not leaving me, do you understand? I don't know what or how you found out about any of those lies, but you need to get it out of your head. I've told you nothing but the truth."

"Get off of her!" D'sani's little voice rang out. She was holding onto the door know with her eyes misting over.

I stopped struggling when I heard her voice and so did Dominic. He looked towards D'sani with a shocked expression on his face. Slowly he moved from off me and sat completely on the bed.

"Who is that?" he stammered.

"Your fucking daughter, you fucking monster!" I yelled.

While Dominic sat on the bed looking confused, I rushed to get dressed and rushed to sweep D'sani in my arms. I rushed downstairs and grabbed the bag that Gloria brought with them, the keys to one Dominic's cars, and headed to the door.

"Wait! Mah'lani! Don't leave! Please!" Dominic pleaded, causing me to pause for a quick second.

I heard his heavy footsteps coming closer and fight or flight entered my body as I opened the door and rushed to the car. Dominic continued to call my name. I securely strapped D'sani in the back seat and hurriedly climbed into the driver seat. My hands trembled as I started the car and pulled away from the house.

"Mama, I wish you were here right now. I need you," I whispered as I drove towards Keana's house.

Surprisingly enough, D'sani was quiet the whole ride, but falling asleep seemed like it wasn't for her. Every time I looked in the rearview mirror, her eyes were bright and open.

I reached Keana's house and parked the car. Going back and forth with myself for a few minutes, I turned the car off and gathered D'sani and her things. My phone kept ringing as I knocked on the door. I knew it was Dominic and I knew he wasn't going to get an answer.

Knock! Knock! Knock!

A few minutes went passed as I waited impatiently for Keana to open the door. D'sani rested her head on my shoulder, bringing me slight comfort.

"Who is it?" I heard Keana say.

"It's me, Kee," I said in a shaky voice, trying to hold it together. The locks were rushed to get the door open. When the door was open, Keana's mouth fell open.

"Lani! What's wrong? Are you okay? Whose baby is this?" Keana fired questions faster than I could answer.

"I will explain everything in the morning. Please let me just get some sleep, please," I begged with tears falling from my eyes.

Keana nodded her head and opened the door wider for us to come in. I went to the guest bedroom and placed D'sani on the bed. I got us undressed and laid down. D'sani snuggled in close to me in bed and we both fell asleep.

Mimi

Chapter Ten

Where there is love, I'll be there
I'll reach out my hand to you, I'll have faith in all you do
Just call my name and I'll be there

"Get up," Keana spoke as she flung the covers from over my body just enough to make sure that D'sani stayed covered. Opening my eyes, I felt pain in my body shooting all over. Keana stood over me with her hands on her hips. I didn't get why she had an attitude, I was the one who just left a dude that I thought I knew.

"What?" I questioned.

"Get up. You need to let me know what is going on. Whose baby did you steal?"

"Can I at least brush my teeth first?"

"Go ahead and meet me downstairs."

Keana left the bedroom as I swung my legs over the bed and got up to go do what needed to be done. After waking up D'sani, I looked for an extra toothbrush and helped her brush her teeth. I looked in her eyes and saw Dominic all over her. How could he deny such a beautiful child?

"Grandma?" D'sani asked as I wiped her face with a clean wash cloth.

"She's not here. You will be with me for a while, okay?"

"Okay. What's your name?"

"Mah'lani. Are you hungry?"

"Yes."

"Let's go eat."

I grabbed D'sani's hand and we walked down to Keana's kitchen where she was in there making breakfast. I helped D'sani get into a chair, fixed her a bowl of oatmeal and myself a cup of coffee. After I took a seat as well, I looked up at

Keana and she was leaning against the counter with her arms folded. Her eyes went to D'sani and back to me.

"Dominic's," I simply said. I really didn't want to talk in front of D'sani because there were things Keana needed to know, but I didn't want to quite say in front of her, even if she did walk in on Dominic beating my ass. She had already seen enough.

"What? How?" Keana asked, showing shock on her face.

"His mom dropped her off yesterday."

"His mother? I thought that she was d-e-a-d," Keana spelled out.

"Yeah, I did too. She showed up all bougie talking about, it's time for Dominic to be a man and take care of his responsibilities. Then she was talking a bunch of hot shit about taking Dominic to court for custody. I told her that she just admitted to a social worker that she didn't want the child any longer. Her defense was that she was surprised that Dominic was into someone like me."

"Someone like you? What the fuck did she mean by that?"

"Me being a big girl. She said he's into thin girls."

"Oh, hell no. Did she leave town yet? 'Cause she 'bout to get an ass whopping that's going to send her to an early grave."

Laughing, I said, "Girl, I would have done that already, but she wasn't worth it."

"You looked a mess last night."

Nodding my head, I stood up and lifted my shirt just to under my boobs and showed Keana the bruises that were forming on my body. They were light right now, but soon they would get darker.

"He's been putting his hands on you? Why the fuck you didn't tell me! Why didn't you leave? What the fuck, Mah'lani?"

"It's not that easy, Keana."

"And why the hell not?"

"This may sound stupid and cliché, but I love him, Keana. I know love isn't supposed to hurt, but he came into my life when I was damn near in shambles."

"I can't believe what you are telling me right now."

"I know what I have to do to make things better and I am willing to work on those things, but - "

Keana slammed her hands against the table, startling myself and D'sani. Tears welled in her eyes as she spoke in a calm, even tone. "No. You don't get to make excuses for him. You don't get to make it seem like he is a knight in shining armor and you are some damsel in distress. You are a strong woman. You don't deserve this. No woman does."

"Don't you think I know that, Keana?" I seethed. I looked at her with red-rimmed eyes and continued. "I have no one besides you and him. So if I must stay to get my shit together and save up to leave, then that's what I'm going to do."

"And what if you can't get out? Then what? What if he decides that he wants to take your life instead of letting you go? What the fuck is everybody who loves you supposed to do? Me, Randy, your father - "

"He is not my father! I have not spoken to that man since my birthday party. Since y'all tried to force him into my life! I didn't want that. Y'all didn't ask me how I would feel! Did anyone think to stop to think about speaking with me first before sneaking behind my back and having little meetings that involve my life!"

"You talk to your boyfriend about that. That was his idea. He thought that he was doing something good. You mad about that, take that up with him."

Licking my lips, I brushed the hair from my face and wanted to say something to Keana. Instead, I stayed quiet.

The door to Keana's house opened and Randy's voice rang out throughout the house. He was talking to Dominic. I dried my eyes as did Keana. D'sani was making a mess out of her oatmeal so I began to clean her up so as to avoid Dominic.

"Who is this cutie pie?" Randy asked when he saw D'sani sitting on my hip.

Dominic adverted his eyes to the floor in shame. My eyes bore a hole in him, wishing that he would acknowledge her just a little bit.

"You can't tell your homeboy's child when you see her? She looks just like him."

Randy looked confused as he looked back and forth from Dominic to D'sani and back again.

"Bro, tell me you haven't been hiding a toddler. Who is her mother? I've been your boy since Pampers."

Dominic sighed, giving me a death stare. I had forced him to do something that he didn't want to: talk about D'sani, like he tried to force Malcolm on me.

"It's a long, complicated story," Dominic spoke.

"And we have the time," Keana replied in a no-nonsense tone. She had one hand on her hip, the other on the table while leaning forward.

D'sani laid her head on my shoulder and I must admit that she was beginning to win me over. Dominic looked over to Keana and Randy, wishing that he was anywhere but there. He was backed into a corner and knew it. I couldn't care less about any of the story. Dominic knew he wasn't going to get out of this one, so he took a seat at the table and began to talk.

Dominic had gotten a girl by the name of Tanya pregnant. She was a stripper and they had unprotected sex only one time, one night. Dominic was on the come-up and every woman that worked at the strip club knew it. Tanya was lucky enough to grab him. He was drunk, and to make sure that he was going home with her, she slipped him an E-pill. They fucked all night and due to his fucked-up state, he didn't care about using a condom. He didn't know anything about Tanya being pregnant until she called him, telling him she was in labor. Tanya didn't die while giving birth. In fact, she was very much alive. Upon D'sani being born, they took a DNA test before Dominic was to sign the birth certificate. The test came back proving that D'sani was, in fact, his child. He signed the birth certificate and began to take care of his responsibilities. Tanya thought she had found her knight in shining armor, but Dominic was strictly there to take care of D'sani. Tanya soon became a bitter baby mother and was making it hard for Dominic to do what he needed to do to be a father.

Dominic ended up coming back to New York after his stay in Atlanta, which was only supposed to last for the weekend. Catching up with his old friends and getting money was what made him stay in New York. Tanya ended up leaving D'sani with his mother and never looked back. Dominic had seen D'sani a few times in the last two years, but the last time was almost a year ago. Gloria told him to stop coming around if he wasn't ready to be there permanently. He chose to make money over being with his child.

"I was going to go back to go get her. I was wrapped up in some things and got caught up," Dominic stated as he dragged his hand down his face.

"When? When she turned eighteen and found out not only did her mother abandon, her but her father did as well? You out here trying to make me forgive my father, but you are doing the same thing to D'sani! And now I see where you get your lying from. Your mother did it so well that I really believed that your child's mother died on the birthing table. It feels like I don't even know you!"

"Mah'lani, I didn't mean to lie to you. I just didn't know how to tell you the truth."

"How about telling it! You know every truth about me because I didn't lie to you. What is there to gain?"

"Nothing, Mah'lani, and I'm sorry."

"Sorry don't mean shit to me. D'sani is the one you need to be apologizing to. I am a big girl and can handle the shit, but that girl will go through life having resentment towards you because you chose money over her! You need to fix this!" I yelled. Tears were evident in my eyes as I looked harshly at Dominic. If I could help it, I refused to let that little girl go through the same thing that I did. Growing up with my mother was amazing, but if I had to admit it, there was the void of my dad missing, and it fucked me up a ton.

I walked out of the kitchen and took a seat on the sofa. My head felt like it was swollen, and it thumped as if someone was banging it with a hammer.

"While we're at it, put your hands on her again, I will have your balls in a fucking martini. Do you fucking hear me? Whatever you need to do to fix this, you need to do so," Keana said.

I chuckled to myself because I knew that I could have counted on her to say something and threaten him all in the same moment.

"You need to mind your business," Dominic said.

"It became my business when you decided to put your hands on her and she told me. Keep your hands off her."

The chair scraped against the kitchen floor and Dominic said, "Randy, get your girl. You need to put a muzzle on her."

"You're a weak man, which is why you're attacking her. Like I said, put your hands on her again and I will be all over your ass."

118

"A'ight, Keana, that's enough. There is already enough going on today," Randy butted in.

"You shut your ass up. That's your friend, do you know how that makes you look? And neither one of y'all niggas tell me shit in my damn house!" Keana yelled and then walked out of the kitchen. Before she walked up the stairs, she swooped D'sani up in her arms and gave me a look that asked if I was okay. I nodded, and she finally went upstairs. Dominic came in the living room soon after.

"Mah'lani, I never meant to hurt you in any way and if I have, I'm truly sorry," Dominic expressed, standing behind me.

"I told you, I'm not the one you need to be apologizing to."

"I know, and I'm going to make sure that I make it up to both of you. I know what I must do and I'm going to fix it. Just please take D'sani home. As a matter of fact, you two spend the day picking out furniture for her room and all new clothes."

The crinkling of money sounded in my ear and I sat up straight in my seat. Dominic placed a bankroll of hundreds in my hands. He kissed my forehead and walked out of the door with Randy hot on his heels.

"You stupid to believe anything that nigga says." Keana's voice resonated in the room.

"Keana, please."

"That's all I'm going to say. But if you come back to me, don't get mad when I tell you I told you so."

Keana left D'sani and her bags with me and went back upstairs. Sighing, I grabbed up D'sani and her things and left Keana's. The mall was our destination.

***

After a long, exhausting day of shopping, D'sani and I were finally back at the house. She was excited and hadn't cried much since Gloria's mean ass had dropped her off. I couldn't have been happier. It seemed like all D'sani did was cry. A little fresh air did the trick and soon a bath before bed would soon follow. D'sani was sitting on the couch while I was in the kitchen making dinner. As I flipped the salmon that was cooking in garlic butter, it hit me that I was forced to step into motherhood. Whether I liked it or not, I vowed that at that moment, I would protect D'sani until I took my last breath.

Heavy footsteps broke me out of my thoughts and I turned my attention to the kitchen doorway. Dominic stood there with stress written all over his face. My heart thundered in my chest so hard that I heard it beating in my ears. Dominic moved closer to me - so close we were exchanging breaths. He held my chin in his hand and squeezed just a tad.

"The shit you pulled today and you leaving last night put a lot of pressure on me. Yes, I fucked up by putting my hands on you, but you know damn well that I love you with everything in my body. Don't you ever pull no shit like that again. Do we have an understanding?" Dominic spoke in a calm tone.

I nodded my head and began to speak, but movement at the door frame caught my attention. It was Malcolm.

"What the fuck is he doing here?" I asked with darkness in my eyes and ice in my tone.

"I invited him to dinner. You made some interesting points this morning and I figured that not only will I repair my relationship with my daughter, you should repair your relationship with your dad. You can at least try with him. I heard the pain in your voice, the pain that you had when you were telling me that I needed to man up and do what I needed to do. Just give it a try for me."

A few eye rolls and huffs and puffs later, I was finishing up dinner and kicking myself in the ass for agreeing with Dominic. Dinner was going to suck, and I had no one to blame except myself for agreeing with Dominic. Malcolm couldn't contain his excitement at the table whereas Dominic didn't so much as look at D'sani. This was going to be harder than I thought. I knew it was going to be some time before he was going to warm up to the thought of being a hands-on daddy, but I wasn't going to leave him any room to change his mind.

"What are you going to do for your birthday?" Malcolm asked Dominic.

With everything that was going on I forgot that Dominic's birthday was about four months away, at the end of August.

"I don't have any ideas because for me. Celebrating my birthday has become overrated. I have everything that I've ever wanted except your daughter as my wife. I'm a patient man so when she is ready is when life will be perfect.

"Mah'lani, have you started making plans for the wedding?" Malcolm asked with a nervous smile on his face.

"No. Too much is going on to be focusing on that. When everything settles, that's when I can focus on that."

And that is how the rest of the dinner went. Malcolm asked questions as I tried to answer as short as possible. Getting close to Malcom was not going to happen easily.

After dinner, Malcolm left, and it was time for D'sani to get bathed and put down for the night. Surprisingly, Dominic offered to do it while I cleaned the kitchen. There was peace in the house. For once.

Mimi

Chapter Eleven

I gave you all of me, but look at us now
Thinking of all your excuses, but they don't add up
Now it's so easy to see, you don't deserve my love

The room spun around me as my body was curled up on the floor. This wasn't normal, but it became normal for me. The pain in my stomach was so bad that there were white lights flashing in front of me. D'sani was crying and I did all that I could to drag my body across the floor. Footsteps echoed through the hall. Sweat was pouring down my neck and face. The pain was so bad that I felt myself losing consciousness.

"Baby! Oh my God!" Dominic yelled upon seeing me on the floor. He came over to me and placed his hand on my head.

I couldn't form any words even if I tried. Dominic's voice began to fade. I slightly heard him screaming into the phone to have an ambulance sent to our home. After that, everything faded to black.

***

I woke up to the sound of beeping. My eyes stayed closed because I heard Dominic on the phone arguing with someone. Damn right I was being nosy, and I didn't care. He had kept a lot of shit from me these past few months and I needed to know what was going on.

"Listen, we gonna have to talk about this another time. I'm at the hospital with my girl right now." He paused to listen to what the person had to say. He continued, "I want you to get rid of it, that's what I want you to do! This was an accident that wasn't supposed to happen, and you need to take care of it." He paused again, exhaling loudly as he listened to the person. He continued, "Look, Diyana, I don't want to be with you. I only fucked you 'cause me and my girl was going through something at the moment and I fucked up. You keep that baby and I promise you will never see that child. Get rid of it or your life will become hell for not listening to what I said. Oh, and do not think about leaving. I have eyes on you and if you even think you gonna flee, it's over for you. So think twice about your decisions. I'll give you until tomorrow to figure out what you gonna do. I'll gladly pay for your abortion."

My heart dropped into the pit of my stomach. I was hurt, to say the least, and the tears tempted to drip from my eyes. I pressed the call button for the nurse and a few moments later, a nurse came inside of the room.

"Ms. Carter, good to see that you are up. You may feel a little groggy because we gave you some pain medication. I am going to check your vitals and let the doctor know that you are awake." The nurse removed proceeded to check my pulse.

Dominic had moved over towards me and tried to hold my hand. I kept my hand balled up and refused to make eye contact.

"Thank you," I said as I tried to scoot back on the bed to lean against it.

"I'm going to go get the doctor for you and he will explain why you are here. Would you like some juice?"

"Yes please."

The nurse smiled at me and walked out of the room.

"How are you feeling?" Dominic asked, yet again trying to hold my hand.

"I feel okay. Where is D'sani?"

"She's in the waiting room with Keana."

"Can you get Keana?"

"Sure. Are you sure that you are okay?"

"Positive," I expressed with a smile on my face.

124

Dominic returned the smile and placed a kiss on my forehead. He walked out of the room to get Keana.

My mind was still tripping about the conversation that I overheard by Dominic. *What the fuck am I supposed to do?* I found myself thinking.

Moments later, Dominic came back with Keana and D'sani. A smile spread across my face when I saw D'sani. Her eyes lit up when she saw me.

"Mama!" she exclaimed, throwing me for a loop.

This was the first time she had called me that and my heart fluttered. She reached her arms out to me and Keana placed her on the bed next to me. Her little arms flew around my neck as she tightly squeezed me.

"Hey, little girl," I addressed D'sani.

"Hi," she responded with her face buried into my neck.

"I'm going to go back to the waiting room to go speak with Randy about something. I'll be back in a few," Dominic said as he made a beeline for the door.

Once he was gone, I spoke. "I bet he do gotta talk to Randy about something."

"What you mean?" Keana asked, taking a seat in the chair that was next to my hospital bed.

"I overheard a conversation that he was having. He must have thought that I was still sleeping. He cheated on me. He got another b-i-t-c-h p-r-e-g-n-a-n-t."

Keana's mouth dropped as she gasped in shock. When the shock wore off, she said, "The nerve of him. How dare he? Mah'lani, what you going to do?"

"Honestly, I don't know. Right now, I need to worry about my health and find out why the fuck I'm in here. I'll deal with his ass later."

"Wow. I can't. This nigga portrayed himself to be some good guy and he nothing but a fuck boy. I should have known since back when you had come to my house that day."

"Language, Keana. D'sani is at the age where she is going to start picking things up."

"I'm sorry, but this is straight bullshit. You stepped up and started taking care of his daughter and this is how he gives you his thanks?"

"I know, Keana. I'm gonna figure out what I'm gonna do. But like I said, I need to figure what's wrong with me so that I could know what it is that I could do to make sure that I take care of myself."

At that moment the doctor walked into the room with Randy, Dominic, and Malcolm. I rolled my eyes at the balloons and flowers that he had. With my chart opened the doctor spoke. "Hello, Ms. Carter. How are you feeling?"

"I still feel a little bit tired. I guess I will be okay."

"Good. Your vitals are good but in the process of doing your bloodwork and running tests, we found out that you have a few small stomach ulcers. While they are painful, they are still small to where if you change your diet and stress less, you should be fine," the doctor said with a smile on his face.

"Is there a way that you could refer her to see a nutritionist? Only because I want to make sure that she eats properly. I want her to have my child and it's already hard with all her missing parts. I want to make sure that she is as healthy as she can be when that time comes," Dominic blurted out.

All eyes were on him as the room grew quiet. Missing parts? Is that what he said?

The doctor cleared his throat and said, "Besides Ms. Carter's stomach ulcers, she is relatively healthy. The fact that she has had both ovaries and fallopian tubes removed makes

126

it harder already for Ms. Carter to conceive. Ms. Carter will get pregnant when her body is ready."

"Does she need to lose weight?" Dominic asked.

"Dominic!" Keana exclaimed. The look on her face said that she was quickly becoming annoyed with his line of questioning.

The doctor was too because he showcased a fake smile on his face. "No, she doesn't. Ms. Carter, I'm going to run a few more tests on you just to cover all bases. When the results come back, you will be free to go home. Try not to stress much. I will prescribe you some Prilosec and refer you to one of the best nutritionists that I know."

I placed a smile on my face and thanked the doctor. I was beyond embarrassed, and Keana glared at Dominic with hatred on her face. Who did think he was? I wanted nothing more than to leave the hospital and go home.

"Let me talk with you for a minute," Randy said to Dominic.

Dominic hesitated at first, but reluctantly followed Randy out into the hall.

Keana grabbed D'sani up from my lap and sat on one of the chairs to watch the Cartoon Network.

Malcolm found his way to the side of the bed and my eyes immediately rolled.

"Listen, I know there isn't much communication between us and I get that you hate my guts, but I see that nigga is not treating you the way you supposed to be treated. The shit that he said was beyond foul and if you need me to take care of it, I gladly will. You are still my daughter at the end of the day and I love you, despite what I did and how you think of me. Is he putting his hands on you?" Malcolm asked.

For the first time since he'd been back, I felt something. "No," I lied.

"You better stop that lying, Mah'lani," Keana spoke from where she was sitting.

"Keana!" I exclaimed.

"Keana my ass. You lucky I didn't let Randy beat his ass that day you came to my house late at night with D'sani. Friend or not, he would have kicked Dominic's ass if I let him. He didn't because I told him not to until you ask for help."

"Keana, D'sani is sitting right in your lap."

"She's asleep."

Malcolm looked at me and dropped his head. "Don't worry, I'm gonna take care of it. Trust me. I owe you that much. Don't you worry; just give me some time."

Everything in my body wanted to protest, but my mind was screaming no. Malcolm placed the balloons on the side of my bed, the flowers on the table, and placed a kiss on my head before he walked out of the room.

Slowly, I began to feel a headache coming on. I just wanted to disappear.

Randy came back inside without Dominic and for that, I was grateful. I didn't know if I was going to be able to deal with him at that moment.

***

Finally, I was home, and with medication, the doctor said that I would be okay. With Dominic gone, my doctor told me that he saw cases of domestic violence and advised me to leave before I ended up on a slab in the basement with a toe tag. He apologized for his bluntness, but he said that was the only way that he could put it.

Nobody could tell me what I knew already. I was fed up and I just wanted to play my cards right. I knew I had to leave this situation, but I refused to let D'sani stay with this broken man. Not one bone in my body would allow me to leave

D'sani. In such a short time D'sani had brought light into my life and she was my savior in human form. Before she came into my life, I knew that I wasn't leaving Dominic for nothing. But D'sani seeing him do those things to me gave me the fight to leave. And I would do that even if it was with my last breath.

Dominic wasn't there when I was being discharged. Randy and Keana came and picked me up from the hospital, telling me that Dominic was out taking care of some things that needed his attention. Of course, my heart was broken, but I told myself not to feel down on myself any more. On the way back home, I asked them to stop at the supermarket so that I could make a special dinner for myself and D'sani. Keana tried to talk to me out of it, but I told her that I needed to do something to keep my mind off reality. Only then did Keana stop bickering with me. Knowing what I wanted to make, I was in and out in less than ten minutes.

Upon entering the house, I knew that Dominic was there not too long ago. His Burberry cologne lingered in the air. Randy brought D'sani in the house, leaving Keana in the car.

"Thank you, Randy. I am going to drop these bags and come out to come get her," I spoke, watching Randy help D'sani take her shoes off.

"It's nothing. I wanted to talk to you anyway."

"About what?"

"Nothing much. I just wanted to thank you for accepting D'sani. Any other woman would have ignored her and proba- bly would have mistreated her, but you treat her as if she is your own. You've done it in such short time, and I commend you. I know my nigga has told you some lies, and I won't even begin to make any excuses for him and why he lied, but he loves you. I know this, but I also know that if he puts his hands on you again, it's lights out."

A smile spread across my face. I said, "What type of social worker would I be if I just ignored D'sani? All she did was be born into this world. She didn't ask to be here. She's saving me while I saved her from her grandmother."

Randy smiled at me, took me into a hug, and left.

I've got to be strong, I repeated to myself in my head. I put D'sani in the tub, washed her up, and placed her in her favorite Mickey Mouse pajamas. After she was done, I did the same for myself.

My phone was going off when I stepped foot out of the tub, and by the bell sound, I knew what it was: messages from Dominic. I took extra time to answer. Dish him the same he dished me.

12:06 P.M. Dominic: Sorry I couldn't make it to pick you up. I had some important issues that I had to deal with.

12:10 P.M. Dominic: I won't be staying out tonight I miss both you and D'sani and I just want to cuddle up with y'all and watch Disney movies all night.

12:26: Dominic: Yo why the fuck you not answering?

12:27: Dominic: Yo!

12:28: Dominic: I swear to God if you don't answer me, you will regret every minute that passed, and you didn't answer me.

12:32 Me: I got into the house not too long ago. I washed D'sani and myself and am just now finishing. I hear what you saying.

12:35 Dominic: I don't give a shit what you are doing. Always have your phone turned on and at your side always.

12:40 Me: Okay, Dominic.

12:43: I got shit to do. Have dinner on the table by 5 o' clock. I'll be there."

12:43 Me: Oh, I already planned to have dinner cooked.

Dominic never answered my last message. I was fine with that. I needed time to think. Nothing that I had with Dominic meant anything. My ache and need for freedom were clawing at me. I could easily leave, but everything in my spirit was telling me to stay a little while longer.

Inside the kitchen while D'sani watched *Paw Patrol* on the couch, I chopped up onions, celery, carrots, garlic, and peppers for the beef stew that was going to be for dinner. I took my time with this meal. Everything was cooked to perfection by the time Dominic came home. The lines in his head told me that he was stressed and just for a quick moment, my heart went out to him. Just a quick moment, because the thought of him cheating on me and getting another chick pregnant flooded my mind.

Dominic walked into the bathroom by the kitchen and washed his face and his hands. I was putting the finishing touches on the rice, squeezing a little lemon juice and parsley. D'sani was in her booster table seat, waiting to eat. Bringing the pots to the table, I took our plates one by one and made them. At this time, Dominic was back at the table.

"Bring me a beer, Mah'lani," Dominic calmly said.

Like a good girl I went into the kitchen, grabbed the beer for him, and gave it to him.

"How was your day?" I managed to ask as I took my seat.

"Stressful, babe. Sometimes I wish that I wasn't the nigga that everybody comes to."

"What happened?"

"Nothing in particular. Today it just felt like everybody had their hands out more than usual today. Everybody's burdens became mine today."

"Well, that's what happens when you are the person who is in charge. You can tell them no so that all that weight isn't on your shoulders. I'm pretty sure that nine times out of ten they are adults and they could handle a no."

"And then I'm the bad guy. It doesn't work like that," Dominic said while placing a heaping amount of beef stew onto his spoon.

"Well, maybe you can change that." I watched as his eyes lit up with enjoyment.

"This is good, babe. This has to be the best beef stew I've ever had."

"I'm glad that you are enjoying it."

For the remainder of dinner, it was quiet. Dominic enjoyed the beef stew and had a second plate while I gathered the left-overs to put them away and clean up. I did so with a smile on my face.

"Hey, babe. Have you thought about when you want to set the date for the wedding?"

"Actually, I have been thinking about it. I was thinking maybe a middle of the fall wedding so it's not too hot or too cold. I'm trying to look cute for our wedding and show off my dress. What do you think?"

"I like the idea. Start planning and sending out invites. The combination for the safe that is in the laundry room behind the dryer is 42-6-13-12-80. There should more than enough in there to take care of what you need to. There is also an address book in my desk drawer in the den with all my closest friend and associates. Send invites to them as well."

"I'll be right on it in the morning. I just want to get D'sani to bed and call it a night. My body is tired." I gathered D'sani in my arms and as I walked past Dominic, he grabbed my arm so that I could face him.

"I don't tell you this enough and I feel lousy that I don't, but I love you, Mah'lani. I can't tell you how much it means to me that you took D'sani and treat her as if she is your own.

I promise that I will make things different. I realized how much of a shitty person, boyfriend, and fiancé I was to you and I will fix what's broken for you, for us, so that we can be a better us."

My heart beat in my chest as those words shook my soul. I wanted to believe it, but I knew that what he was saying was only his way of making himself feel better. That's what he always did. And I was tired of it.

"I love too, babe," I responded as I placed a kiss on his lips.

Dominic took D'sani from my arms and stood up. "I'll go with D'sani. Tuck her in and read her a book. You go relax in a bubble bath."

"Are you sure?"

"Yes. I must start doing this with D'sani and forming a bond with her. I've been so busy and neglecting my family as it is. That has to change."

"Okay."

I was a bit skeptical, but I made my way upstairs and ran a bath with lavender and eucalyptus bath salts and lavender bubble bath. I lit candles and placed them around the bathroom. I went back inside the bedroom to grab a book from the bookshelf, and I paused as I heard D'sani's laughter and Dominic mimicking the giant from Jack and the Beanstalk. With a smile on my face, I turned back and went to enjoy my bubble bath.

***

The next morning, I got up and made breakfast and got ready for my day. D'sani was going to be going to daycare, I was headed to work, and Dominic was going to be out taking care of what he had to. For once in my life, things felt normal.

We had breakfast together, we dropped D'sani off together, and then Dominic dropped me off at work.

"I don't know if I will be done by the time you get off of work," Dominic mentioned.

"It's okay. I'll take an Uber."

Dominic placed a kiss on my lips as I got ready to climb out of the car.

Keana texted me as I made my way inside with an address and told me to meet her there for lunch. I agreed and made my way to get my work done. Today wasn't a field day for me so I sat at my desk, immersed deeply in my cases and going over them twice to make sure that I didn't miss anything.

Around ten-thirty I got distracted. I heard Clarissa's voice and another female's voice that wasn't recognizable. Clarissa was telling the woman that she shouldn't be there and that the woman needed to leave. At first the woman was quiet about it, but soon it began to escalate. I got up from my seat and went to go see what the chaos was about.

"Clarissa, everything all right over here?" I asked.

The woman who was talking shit was beautiful. Like model beautiful. Her chestnut brown hair glistened with natural shine and flowed down her back. She was rocking diamonds in her ears, on her neck, around her wrists, and on her fingers. Her almond-shaped green eyes held mystery, but made her look exotic as well. She was dressed in a Fendi sundress that stopped above her knee and stuck to her every curve. On her feet were open-toed Giuseppe heels and her toes painted to perfection.

"Yes, Mah'lani. I'm just waiting on security to get up here," Clarissa responded.

Ole girl stopped yelling when she noticed that Clarissa stopped talking to her.

"Mah'lani?" the woman asked.

The way she spat my name, you would think that she knew me and had beef with me for years.

"Do I know you?" I asked. By now people were recording the exchange on their phone and recording live on Facebook, as if they weren't at work.

"Nah, I don't know you, but bitch, you finna know these hands if you don't tell me where the fuck my daughter and my baby father at!" she yelled.

"Tanya?"

"Bitch, yes! Tell me where the fuck they at so I can bring they asses home. Nobody told Gloria's old ass to bring my daughter up here no way! When I'm done with your ass, I'm going back to Atlanta and whopping her old ass!"

Tanya was on fire. She was trying to get around Clarissa and one of my co-workers. Security finally arrived, and they dragged her out of the office.

"Mah'lani, in my office, and whoever recorded that, keep the recording. If you delete it before it gets to be used as evidence, you will be fired," Clarissa threatened.

I followed Clarissa into her office and took a seat while she paced back and forth.

"Before you say anything, I don't know that woman. I only know from a story I was told," I explained.

"Tell me from the beginning so I can know what steps I need to take while dealing with this."

For ten minutes, I explained to Clarissa everything that had been going on in my life. Holding tears along the way. Clarissa gripped me into a hug and told me that everything would be okay. Clarissa told me to take the rest of the day off and assured me by the next morning things would be handled.

On my way out of the office building, I texted Keana to see if she was free. Within moments, she replied and told me that I could swing by the group home that she worked at.

The Uber that I requested was patiently waiting as my feet softly hit the pavement. I battled with myself as to whether or not I should tell Dominic about what had happened. This morning was the first day in a long while that we were peaceful, and I didn't want to fuck it up. Shaking my head, I dialed the day care that D'sani was at to check on her. If Tanya knew where I worked, there was a possibility that she could have found out where D'sani was. To my relief, they connected me to her teacher and she confirmed that they just finished eating lunch and they were about to take a nap. I thanked her teacher and enjoyed the drive to Keana's job.

"Ms. Carter, Ms. Carter," the front desk clerk said once he saw me. His smile flashed brightly, his facial hair glistened under the lights, and his chocolate skin was radiant.

"Hey, Nolan. How are you?" I asked with a polite smile on my face.

"I'm well, and yourself?" His eyes wandered over my body and landed on my eyes.

"Good. These teenage girls driving you crazy today?"

"Surprisingly, it's quiet today. All of them went to school today. I think it's gonna rain cats and dogs because that is a miracle. I'm quite sure that it's going to go down in flames when they get back in here. I feel bad for the night crew." Nolan chuckled.

I joined in with him because Nolan's laugh is the kind that makes you join in whether you want to or not.

"You are crazy. I needed that laugh. Where's Keana?"

"Her raggedy ass back there in her funky-ass office. Let me walk you back there."

"Leave my best friend alone. Y'all friendship is ridiculous."

"That's 'cause she rude and snappy like she some old rich white man's wife."

I threw my head back in laughter. I said, "You ain't right."

"You know, I've been wanting to ask you something for a minute."

"What's that?"

Nolan looked nervous, but then he puffed his chest out and said, "I was wondering if it was cool if I took you out to dinner. I find you to be a very attractive woman and if I have to admit it, I've been crushing on you since the moment you walked through those doors almost a year ago."

My mouth dropped because I never thought that he was even checking for me. When it came to Dominic, my eyes were only for him, and if it was any other men that was checking for me, I didn't notice.

"If I was a single woman, I would take you up on your offer. I am actually engaged," I said softly and raised my left hand.

"Oh, I'm sorry. I never realized that you were. He must be the luckiest and happiest man alive. Any dude would have to be with you on his arm."

I blushed a tad bit and thought about what he said. I didn't think Dominic felt that way at all. Up until recently, I didn't know exactly what he was thinking and how he felt.

"Thank you for your kind words, Nolan," I responded with a smile on his face.

Keana's door swung open and she stood there looking at us.

"What's up, Kee?" Nolan said to annoy Keana. He knew that the only one allowed to call her Kee is me.

"Get your ass back to the front desk, Nolan."

"Leave him alone, Keana. He was just walking me to your office."

"You know where it's at."

"Ahh, you just a hater," Nolan said, sticking his tongue out at Keana.

"A hater for what?"

"'Cause I'm fine as hell and you not."

Keana started in his direction and I held her back. Nolan speed-walked backwards down the hall as Keana yelled, "Take your childish ass back up front!"

As I made it inside Keana's office, I was cracking up. She said, "One day, I'm gonna bust that nigga in his house something good."

"Leave him alone; he's harmless."

"Like hell he is. Always being childish. Anyway, what are you doing here so early?"

"Clarissa sent me home for the rest of the day."

"For what? Are you okay?"

"Yeah, I'm cool. I'd rather show you then tell you." I took my phone out of my handbag and searched one of my co-workers who recorded the incident with Tanya. I found the video with ease and passed the phone to Keana. Her mouth dropped as she watched the video in shock.

"How the fuck did she find out where you work?" Keana asked.

"I have no clue. Clarissa said that she was going to handle it."

"Did you let Dominic know?"

"No. We had a great morning. The first in a long time. And I don't want to fuck it up by telling him at least not until we are face to face."

Keana rolled her eyes and said, "You don't need to feel like you gonna fuck anything up. He has done you so much fucked up shit to you in such little time. Are you afraid of him?"

Was I? To be honest, I didn't know how to answer that question. When he would have his mood swings, of course in that moment, I was scared. The tears slid down my face with ease. I wiped them away. I was tired of crying. I was tired of feeling sorry for myself.

"I fed him dog food," I blurted out.

"What?" Keana asked.

"You know how when I came home from the hospital and I asked if Randy could stop at the grocery store?"

"Yes."

"I made two separate pots of beef stew that night. One was for me and D'sani and the other was for Dominic. I mixed some beef chunks to his so that he wouldn't be suspicious. He still doesn't know."

Keana was silent for the moment and then released a laugh so hearty you would have thought she was at a Def Comedy Jam show. She laughed so hard that she had a hard time breathing.

"Bitch! What? I can't fucking take you," she finally responded while wiping tears from her face.

"He's hurt my heart so much that I felt like I needed to do something for revenge. Something that he wouldn't find out. Now that I did it, it doesn't bring me much joy because he doesn't know."

"Get your things and let's go."

"Where are we going?"

"To the address I sent you."

"What is it?"

"You'll see when we there. Shut up with your questions. Oh, and you have to let Nolan take you out to dinner. Besides him being petty with me, he's a decent guy and someone you need to be with."

"Keana - "

"Keana my ass. Shut up and let's go."

Rolling my eyes at her, I gathered my things and followed Keana. Twenty minutes later we arrived at an office building that had a sign that said Helping Her in purple lettering. I looked at Keana with a side and still followed her lead and got out of the car. We walked inside and up to the desk.

"Welcome to Helping Her. Do you have an appointment today?" the woman behind the desk asked with a smile on her face.

"Yes. I'm here to see Quinn."

"Okay, have a seat and I will let her know. What is your name?"

"Keana Richards."

We took a seat and not even a good five minutes later, a beautiful woman with thick, golden-brown, curly hair came around the corner, sporting a pregnant belly that looked like she was ready to pop.

"Hi, Keana. I'm glad that you could make it. You two ladies can come on back."

"I wouldn't have missed this meeting for the world," Keana expressed.

I looked on, wondering what the hell was going on.

It was quiet walking down to Quinn's office. There were pictures of women, some with women, some not. There were short stories under the pictures that I couldn't read. I didn't want to linger behind.

"Y'all can have a seat. You must be Mah'lani. My name is Quinn, and it's nice to meet you."

"I would like to say the same thing, but I don't even know what's going on," I responded.

Keana turned to me with a serious look on her face and my heart dropped to the pit of my stomach. She took my hands into hers and began, "Mah'lani, Quinn is a survivor of domestic violence. Her story is remarkable. From my perspective, I can't imagine what you go through with Dominic, but I know that you don't deserve it. There are so many women who are in these situations and it either ends with them being murdered, in suicide, or they survive. I don't want you to be murdered, nor do I need you to commit suicide. You are my sister, and I refuse to let anything to happen to you. I brought you here to hear Quinn's testimony in hopes that it helps more than I can. You mean the world to me, so you know I can't lose you. Quinn also has counselors here, but I will let her explain it all to you herself. You are a strong woman, so I know that you will listen to what she has to say. I know you're tired of being Dominic's punching bag. It's all in your eyes, and I'd rather help you than to help myself to jail for killing this nigga."

What did I do to deserve such a good friend? All I could do is nod my head. Keana hugged me and placed a kiss onto my cheek. This was an intervention of some sort and I could only accept it. She was seeing something that I couldn't see. So many women didn't have this opportunity with someone helping them to seek help.

Keana exited the room and left me with Quinn. The hour that I spent in that room with Quinn brought more tears to my eyes. She told me her story and I told her mine. My story wasn't as bad as hers, but her body and soul cried just as hard as mine did when she told me her story. My heart was heavy when I left, but my mind was clear. I knew what I needed to do. I thanked Keana all the way to pick up D'sani up and back home.

"You know I got you, girl, and if you want to go back, I'll be there holding your hand along the way. I love you, sister," Keana expressed.

"I love you too," I spoke softly and got out of the car. Dominic's car was in the driveway. I exhaled and looked at Keana, who was looking at me with a knowing look.

"If you need me, call me," she said.

"We had a good day, so we should be fine."

"It doesn't matter. There is no telling what kind of mood he could be in."

I gave Keana the smile that white people give black people when they feel uncomfortable around us. I gave her a hug and made my way in the house.

The house was dark and quiet, with just slivers of the setting sun coming through spaces in between the curtains. I took D'sani upstairs to her room and peeked into our bedroom along the way and noticed Dominic. He was laid out on the bed with his shoes off and mouth cocked open. *Thank God,* I thought. I proceeded to get D'sani ready for a bath. Dinner was going to be getting ordered tonight, due to my tiredness.

By the time the food had gotten delivered, I heard Dominic moving around upstairs. D'sani was already seated at the table as I fixed our plates and waited for Dominic to come down. He was now out of his outside clothes and sported just pajama pants and socks. His body almost made me drool on myself. I tried to remember the last time that we had sex. My eyes ate him up and I bet if D'sani wasn't there, I would have sucked his dick right there at the table.

"Are you okay?" Dominic's voice boomed, jerking me from my impure thoughts.

"Yes. Just admiring your body. It's been a while."

"I know, babe. Shit's just been hectic."

"Daddy," D'sani interrupted.

"Yes, baby girl."

"I want juice."

"You have to eat some more of your food before you can get some," Dominic answered.

D'sani was about to have a full-on temper tantrum, but one look from Dominic and she continued to eat. I giggled and shook my head. Even the little bit of time she had been around her father, she knew not to try it.

"How was your day?" Dominic asked me while placing some curry noodles on his fork.

"Informative, to say the least."

"Really?" he questioned with a raised brow.

"Yes. Tanya thinks that she was gonna waltz into New York and think that she's just gonna take you and D'sani back to Atlanta."

Dominic stopped eating his food and looked up at me. He asked, "What the fuck do you mean? Tanya?"

I reached for my phone and decided to show him. He accepted my phone and watched the video. His eyes darkened, and I just knew that our night was going to take a turn for the worse.

"Clarissa said that she would take care of everything. My thinking, she's gonna put in an emergency order for us to say that we have physical and sole custody of D'sani. I won't actually know until I get to work tomorrow."

"I'm gonna kill this bitch," Dominic growled.

"You didn't know that she was up here?"

"Nah. Nobody up here knows what she looks like except Randy and he would have told me if he saw her. Damn, man!"

"Babe, don't worry about it. She won't be able to do anything with D'sani. Not without a fight. She basically abandoned D'sani and - "

"I'm not worried about her coming back for D'sani. That's not what she's doing. It's me that she wants, and it's you I'm concerned with."

"Me?" I asked. *What the fuck for? I know how to handle myself!*

"Yes, you. That woman is manipulative and crazy. She's not going to stop until she gets what she wants."

"In case you didn't know, I don't play when it comes to the people that I love. I may not be a fighter, but I will fight if I'm pushed enough. You should know that much. After all, that's how you met me in the first place. If it's a fight that she wants, then that is exactly what she is going to get. From the story that you told me, I've been more of a mother to D'sani than she has."

Dominic exhaled. The look on his face said that he wanted to drop the subject, so I did. We continued our dinner in silence.

I could tell Dominic was thinking. Hell, I was too. Tanya had another thing coming to her if she thought she was just going to come all the way to New York and take something that she never had.

As I cleaned up our mess, Dominic came into the kitchen to let me know that he was stepping out for a few and not to wait up for him. So much for us having sex when D'sani went to bed. I did not respond to Dominic, and when the door closed, I locked up for the night. Exhausted, I made my way upstairs to bathe myself and D'sani and call it a night.

Chapter Twelve

And you got me like, let go
What you want from me?
And I tried to buy your pretty heart,
But the price too high

In the middle of a nap, I heard Dominic's footsteps heavily against the floor. His footsteps were rushed coming up that stairs as if he was on a mission. My eyes remained closed because I knew that he was back on some fuck shit. We had had a full week of us being on good terms, like how things were in the beginning. I knew that it was too good to be true.

The doorknob to the bedroom twisted and in walked Dominic. His heavy breathing and the stench of alcohol filled the room as he walked to his side of the bed where D'sani was sleeping, picked her up, and walked back out of the room. While I still acted like I was asleep, on the inside, my body was warning me that something wasn't right. My heart was beating out of my chest, damn near on the bed next to me. I even felt a little trickle of sweat running down my lower back.

Dominic came back inside of the room, but I couldn't tell what he was doing. The tug at my pants excited me because lately I had been frustrated sexually. The heat from his fingers were like little bolts of electricity igniting something in me. His lips soon joined his hands as he placed kisses on my legs. The heat between my legs was so intense that if I moved and caused any friction, a fire was bound to start. The further up his kisses went, the wetter I became. Dominic turned me onto my back as I opened my eyes and looked down at him. My panties came off - no, scratch that, he ripped them off. His tongue was now on my swollen clit, my legs over his shoulders, and my hand palming his head.

My juices leaked from his chin and between my ass cheeks. My hands lifted my shirt and pulled my breasts from my bra. Biting down on my lip, I used my fingers to pinch and caress my nipples. Dominic's fingers found my opening and slid in with ease and my hips grinded down on them as if it was his dick inside of me.

"Mmm. Dominic, I'm ready to cum," I moaned.

My body began to shake, and I couldn't control it. This was the most powerful, body-shaking, orgasm that I was about to experience. And this fool stopped. His eyes penetrated mine as I looked down at him with a wild look in my eyes. He climbed up my body and rested on his knees between my legs to take his shirt off. My pussy was throbbing and at that point, I just wanted to cum. Dominic kissed my lips with my juices still on his lips and beard. Swiftly his pants and boxer briefs were off. I pushed him onto his back on the bed and climbed on top of him. His dick was hard under me, now coated with my love.

"That wasn't fair," Dominic said as I planted my feet on the bed, balancing myself above his dick, which stood straight up. All eight inches of pure, veiny, thickness.

"It stopped being fair when you decided to abruptly stop me from cumming," I responded with my eyes trained on him.

Wrapping my hand around his manhood, I guided him inside me with a moan, satisfied that he was now where I longed for him to be. He grabbed my waist as I started off with slow, even bounces that matched his thrusts. I came instantly, but it wasn't as powerful as I knew it would have been if his mouth was still on me.

Sweat formed on my brow and lower back as I sped my pace up and Dominic's thrusts got deeper. His hands were on my ass cheeks, helping me slide up and down on his dick. The sound my pussy made excited us both as I came again, my love now on his stomach and thighs.

Dominic placed his hand on my lower back and flipped me under him, his dick never leaving my body. His lips softly graced my shoulder and his hand softly squeezed my neck, bringing ecstasy into my life.

"I love you," Dominic whispered in my ear.

I couldn't respond with his dick digging in me. His strokes were long and deep, and I knew he was just about ready to cum. His grunts rang in my ear, and as he grabbed onto my shoulders, I threw this pussy on him, even if I was under him. Moments later he was spilling his seeds inside of me. We both collapsed, trying to regain our breathing. Sleep called me.

Baby you got me like oh
You love when I fall apart
So, you can put me together
And throw me against the wall

Splash!

I sat up right in the bed as cold water connected with my body. I tried to process what the fuck was going on, but my skin lit up with fire as the sting from a belt connected with my body. I dipped and dodged, all the while trying to figure out what was going on. Dominic's eyes were wild as his arms moved so fast I thought he had eight of them. My screams did nothing for him because he didn't let up. Finally getting my brain cells together, I dodged from the bed and landed on the floor, opposite Dominic.

"You filthy, fat bitch! You thought your ass was slick, but I'm going to show your ass one way or another!" Dominic yelled, dropping the belts walking out of the room.

The floodgates opened as I looked over my body. The welts were evident on my skin already and bright red. Getting up from the floor, I went to the closet to put clothes on. As I reached for the doorknob, I paused to look for my cell phone. It was nowhere in sight. I needed to call for help. This was my last straw. I didn't know what I could possibly have done to deserve this. We were just making the sweetest love that we've ever had and now this.

"What the fuck?" I expressed as I tried to open the door. I couldn't get it open. It must have been locked from the outside.

The door took my assault as I kicked and punched the door without it even budging. I even threw my hip and shoulder into it. My body shook like an earthquake as I realized D'sani was out there with a monster of a daddy. Leaning against the wall, I slid to the floor with a new set of tears falling from my eyes. This was my end, and I felt it all through my bones.

The sunlight went down, and it was now dark, and Dominic still hadn't returned. The silence killed me, and not knowing if D'sani was okay was putting me straight into a coffin. I sat in the same spot for as long as I could and then I made my way to the bed. There was nothing that I could use to break the door open. Just as I thought I had a plan, there were keys jingling against the door knob and Dominic walked into the room. My body still ached as I slid off the bed and away from him.

"Why did you do that to me?" I asked. I trembled with fear. If he could wet me and beat me, not with one, but two belts, there was no telling what he could do after that.

"What is this?" he asked calmly as he held out an opened can of dog food.

I could kick myself because I remember hiding the can under the sink. I was supposed to remember to throw it out when

I began to clean up our mess, but it totally slipped my mind, and now this is what I had to deal with.

"Dog food, babe," I responded with a knot stuck in my throat.

"Why the fuck was it under the fucking sink, opened? We don't have a dog, Mah'lani!"

"One day there was a d-dog in our b-backyard. I went to the store and b-bought a can of food for it. I p-put it under the sink to save it for later that day, to give the dog the r-rest. I guess I forgot."

Dominic laughed and said, "You aren't a good liar, babe. This can is fucking empty! What did you do with it? This shit looks mighty close to the beef stew you made, so tell me, Mah'lani, did you feed this bullshit to me?"

I had two options. One, I could lie and say no, but I just stuttered through the first lie and he saw right through that. Two, tell him the truth and just accept whatever he was going to do me when I did. Dominic began to slowly come my way and fear settled in yet again.

"I did feed it to you! We've barely been together for a year and three months and you have done everything to me that I vowed to myself to never accept from a nigga! You've abused me physically, verbally, and emotionally and I needed to do something to feel like I did something! You've lied to me about your mother and your child - your child, who doesn't deserve a father like you! You were a coward and did nothing but throw money around and called it 'taking care of her'. You cheated on me with God knows who and got her pregnant! Yeah, I bet you didn't think I knew that! You are the reason why females wish that y'all niggas come with a caution sign!" I belted. I was tired of being silent. I was tired of him thinking it was okay for him to do whatever to me. Tonight, it was going to end, and I was leaving with D'sani on my hip. Whether he was the father or not.

Dominic stalked my way and when he reached me, he grabbed me by the back of my neck and dragged me. This wasn't about to be easy for him. Granted, he was bigger than me, but I was going to fight back. I thought about Quinn's story and how she fought back against her abuser, Jason, and it gave me strength. I spun out of Dominic's grasp, but he was on me again pulling me by my hair.

"Oh, you think it's a game? Bring your ass on!" he yelled.

"Ahh! Somebody help! Help me!" I yelled and continued to yell as he pulled me towards the stairs. At the top, he paused and back-handed me, busting my lip wide open. Blood splashed onto the wall and leaked onto the floor.

"See what the fuck you made me do!"

Yeah, like I was the problem. Dominic pushed me to the floor and yanked me towards the stairs by my leg. I just knew what was about to happen and I couldn't afford to get dragged down the stairs.

"No! Let me go, Dominic! Nooo!"

My screams went unheard because he still proceeded to drag me. I did everything I could to stop him, but nothing worked. Eventually my body slid and banged against the wooden stairs. It was a few seconds, but with each bump and bang, it felt like hours.

"All you had to do was comply. All you had to do was be my bitch! We are getting married soon and you want to feed me dog food! I only loved you. Took you in when your ugly-ass mama died, and this is the thanks that your fat ass gives me!" he yelled.

My voice had turned hoarse from screaming so much. As he dragged me to the kitchen, D'sani once again popped up in my head.

"Where is D'sani?" I asked amid his yelling. I kicked him with all my might with my free foot, landing the blow behind his knee. Instantly, his tall ass fell to the floor with a bang.

"Argh!" he yelled.

I took the chance to get up from the floor. I ignored the pain and ran as fast as I could to the door. My hand was on the knob when I was yanked and thrown against the wall. Dominic placed his hand around my throat and made me stand up. He spewed words of hatred to me as he forced me to walk to the kitchen. The floor was cold on my face as he slung me to the floor.

"Dominic, please," I begged.

"Please, my ass! You fucked up by feeding me that shit. I wondered why, for that entire night, my stomach was fucked up. I thought you did something, but then I thought you couldn't be that damn stupid. And you know what? I was right. If you would have just thrown the can away, you would have gotten away with it." He laughed like a madman.

"Where is D'sani?"

"Oh, don't worry, she's not here. Ever since she showed up, you stopped catering to me. Ooh, but you're going to pay."

My head swirled with pain, confusion, and cloudiness. Dominic moved around the kitchen and dared me to move. My eyes never left him and for the first time, I was seeing him clear as day. He was the devil in human form, I was sure of it. He broke my thoughts when he dropped a bowl in front of me that contained dog food.

"What is this?" I asked.

"The same shit you fed me. Just not disguised in beef stew. Eat it. Now!"

I looked up at Dominic in disbelief. He couldn't be serious. The look on his face told me otherwise. Moments of silence passed with us looking at each other. He kneeled and looked at me. There was a slight mist in his eyes and for a quick millisecond, I thought he had changed his mind, but then his fist came crashing into my face. He yelled once again for me to eat it and added that it would only get worse if I didn't. No way in hell did I want to find out what was worse, so I began to eat it. I was beyond humiliated. What made it worse was when he told me to get on all fours, like a dog, and eat it without my hands. I did what he said and as fast as I could as to not allow it to linger on my taste buds. My tears and snot mixed in with it. With my last bite, Dominic landed a swift blow to my stomach and everything that I had just consumed was on the floor.

"I should have told that bitch to keep that baby. You know why? 'Cause you can't give me none no matter how hard I try!"

He grabbed me by the hair again and dragged me to the living room. My knees burned against the carpet in the living room and I screamed out in pain. He didn't let go until we were by the couch, and I took that opportunity to punch him in the nuts, causing him to drop to his knees. I stood up with blood, snot, tears, and vomit on my face, I cocked my hand back and decked him as hard as I could. I took flight towards the door and ran outside. My lungs welcomed the fresh air.

"Help! Somebody help me!" I yelled.

I started to run towards the end of the driveway, but yet again, I was too slow. Dominic yanked me by the shirt, placed his hand over my mouth, and walked me back to the house. Inside, he threw me to the floor, locked the door, and dragged me to the kitchen.

"I've only loved your ass! Fed your fat ass with my hard-earned money. Picked you up when you were down! Introduced you to your damn daddy and you took it for granted!" he shrieked. There was pain in his voice and for the life of me, I didn't know why. He had some nerve.

"No! You don't get to feel this way, like I've done so much bad shit to you! You've been treating me like shit for months now. I've been dealing with your fucked-up ways! I did one thing, and you want to act like you are so hurt! I've lost so much weight stressing behind you; my clothes fall over me like blankets. I tried so hard to deal with your lying, cheating, abusive ass, but you have made it impossible!"

Slap!

My head twisted to an awkward angle and pain surged up my neck. I just knew my neck was broken. He didn't even stop at that point. He continued to put his hands on me. Blows landed on the top of my head, my arms, chest, ribs, and back. He didn't stop until I was bloodied and black and blue, crumpled up in the corner. Dominic's face and bald head glistened with sweat as he squatted in front of me. My arm was over my head so that I could block the blow that I knew was coming.

"You listen to me, and listen to me good. You aren't leaving me. You will marry me, you will be a good wife and stepmother to D'sani. This will never happen again if you do what you supposed to do. The only thing that you need to do is clean and do laundry. I don't trust you enough to cook for me, so I will hire some to do so. Clean up your mess!"

I was trapped. How did I live like this and it not be a possibility that my life will end prematurely? I was sure that I was going to die tonight if he didn't stop when he did. Dominic was ready to walk away, but stopped when he realized that he had more to say.

"If you try to call the police or even try to leave, you and your best friend will be in the ground lying next to your rag-gedy-ass mama. Do we have an understanding?"

"Yes," I simply said.

Satisfied with my answer, Dominic left the kitchen, leaving me to clean up all the vomit, blood, and snot that he had knocked out of me.

Must be love on the brain
That's got me feeling this way
It beats me black and blue
But it fucks me so good
And I can't get enough

***

"Keana, I don't know if I want to do this," I muttered as I looked at myself in the mirror, dusting my face with finish stay powder. She had walked in at the right time. I was done hiding the light bruise that sat under my eye. Dominic lied about not abusing me after the time that he made me eat the dog food. In fact, it got worse, and I wore more makeup to cover my bruises to hide them from my co-workers and Keana.

"Why not? Even though I hate his guts, it seems like he stopped being a dick and you love him, right? You seem so much happier since his truth came out, so what could possibly be wrong?" Keana asked as she held the steamer to my dress.

"I don't think I'm ready."

I didn't think. I knew that I wasn't ready. I fell out of love with Dominic after I had to eat the dog food. I was just going with the flow so that neither I nor Keana lost our lives behind this psychopath.

"Oh honey, you're just experiencing cold feet. It'll pass, I'm sure."

I sighed because I knew that it wouldn't go away. I was done with my makeup and went to put my dress on. My dress was white, of course, and had beaded embroidery. The corset was intricately designed to fit my boobs nice and snug without them spilling over the top. The bottom half was ruffled and poofy like a loofah and the train expanded ten feet behind me.

Tires sounded in the driveway and Keana peeked out of the window.

"The limo is here. Come let me help you with your veil."

I turned in her direction as she lifted her arms above my head to make sure that my veil was on right. Our eyes caught each other, and she sniffled.

"Bitch, don't you fucking dare," I said, knowing that she was about to cry.

"How can I not? You look fucking beautiful. Like a princess." Keana burst out in a full-on ugly cry.

"Thank you. That means so much to me. You have to stop before you ruin your makeup," I said, trying to hold back my own tears. Not because I was getting married, but because at that moment, I knew if I didn't comply with Dominic, I would never share any more crying moments with her.

Keana sniffled and used some Kleenex she had in her purse to dab away her tears. "Okay, come on, let's go get you married."

"Give me a second. Let me say a prayer and talk to my mama right quick. Fix your makeup in the limo," I said with a smile on my face.

She smiled and nodded and let me have my moment. The door closed behind Keana and I looked around the bedroom that I shared with Dominic. There was so much love and hate that was held in that room, it was ridiculous. In my wedding dress, I kneeled and bowed my head. I prayed to God and asked him to help me to find it in my heart to forgive Dominic. I asked God to forgive him and to heal his heart, mind, body, and spirit because He knew that Dominic was holding something so traumatic deep inside of him, for him to act the way that he did. I asked for strength to get through this day successfully. I talked to my mama next for a minute or two, letting her know that I loved and missed her tremendously. I also joked and told her to send me a sign if she felt like I was making a complete fool out of myself.

I got off my knees and gathered my train into my arms and made a beeline for the limo. On the ride over to The Water's Edge Lighthouse, where our ceremony and reception were being held, I perspired due to my nervousness. Keana tried her best to keep me calm. She turned to me when we arrived, and she smiled that dumb-ass smile again.

"I am going to go inside and let everyone know that you are here. I'll be back out."

"Just hope that I'm here when you get back," I joked.

She gave me the finger and closed the door, going on her way. She must have taken my joke seriously because out walked Malcolm. He was dressed in a white tuxedo. A turquoise silk shirt rested underneath, he had a white bow tie with turquoise polka dots on his neck, and the same colored shoes on his feet. His hair cut was fresh, and I had to admit that he looked sharp. When he was close to the door, I opened it and allowed him to take my hand. My body unfolded as I stepped onto the curb and his expression shocked me. Almost instantly, he began ugly crying. *Why is everybody doing this to me today?*

"Malcolm, please," I begged. I put my differences aside from all the bullshit that was between us and kept the peace. But shit, I wasn't expecting for him to cry like this.

"I'm sorry. You are so beautiful," he said, drying his eyes with the back of his hands. He continued, "Keana said that you were beautiful, but man. You're angelic. I'm glad that you allowed me to experience this moment."

I didn't respond. I just displayed my smile and allowed Malcolm to hold my hand and walk me to the entrance. There was a piano playing faintly as we walked in and made it to the doors that would lead me to the man who held my life in his hands.

Keana slid through the door and shocked us both. "Are you ready?" Keana asked me, looking at us like we were crazy.

"No, but let's get this is shit done and over with," I answered. Before my foot was in front of my other one, Malcolm softly yanked my hand back, causing me to look at him.

"What do you mean no? This is serious, Mah'lani, and not a game. You need to be sure a hundred percent that this is what you want."

"I said let's do it," I responded without answering Malcolm's question.

"If you don't want to do this, just say the word and we could run out of here together."

"Yeah, right. Like Dominic would let you."

"Don't get it twisted, baby girl. I work for him, but my hands still work and so does my trigger finger. I told you if you need me to handle it, I will."

"That won't be necessary. I got D'sani. Y'all two move to y'all positions. The music is going to begin."

"Keana, you just gonna let her walk down that aisle knowing that she has mixed emotions about it?" Malcolm asked.

"Stop dragging it out. She's just having cold feet. It'll pass when she gets up there." Keana acted like she knew what she was talking about.

Malcolm, giving up the argument, moved out of the way and Beyoncé's "One Plus One" began to play. D'sani walked out first, throwing blue flower petals to the ground as people snapped photos of her in a smaller version of my dress and without the train.

Next were Randy and Keana, who looked at each other as if it was their wedding. I watched them walk down the aisle and averted my attention to Malcolm.

"On my signal, grab D'sani and Keana and get them as far away from the altar as fast as you can."

"Huh? What do you mean? What signal?"

"You'll know."

Next was Malcolm and me. He tried to keep a straight face, but I could tell he was trying to process what I said. My smile was wide, and it appeared to everyone that I was ready. We reached the altar and Malcolm tried to ask me again what I meant, but I ignored him.

"Who gives this woman away?" the reverend asked.

I looked at Dominic, who was sporting his signature pearly white teeth and bald head. He looked good in the same colors that Randy and Malcolm were wearing.

"I do," Malcolm stated and placed my hand into Dominic's. Malcolm looked on, trying to decipher when I was going to give him the signal, and I couldn't help but to die on the inside.

"Is there anyone here today that objects to this holy matrimony? Speak now or forever hold your piece," the reverend asked.

Dominic and I faced the crowd and watched everyone look at each other to make sure no one wanted to interject. Dominic held a grimace on his face. The wind picked up and as clear as day, I heard the word *"leave"* whispered loudly in my ear. I'd been hearing it since I left the house, but I just thought that

I was tripping. Before Dominic and I faced each other, I made eye contact with Malcolm and slightly nodded. He swooped in and grabbed Keana by the hand as she tried to cradle D'sani. Dominic looked on with suspicion and turned his attention towards me.

"I have something to say," I said. The grimace returned to Dominic's face and I knew he wanted to smash my face in. I continued, "I can't do this. I can't marry you, and I'm not even sorry about it. There is something that all of you don't know. Dominic has been abusing me for quite some time and I hid it because I didn't want anyone to know. I was ashamed. He told me if I didn't marry him and be the perfect wife and stepmother, he would put myself and Keana in the ground next to my mother. This is not the person that I want to spend the rest of my life with."

"Mah'lani!" Dominic yelled my name.

"What?" Randy questioned.

"I'm not afraid or ashamed anymore. Dominic, as of this morning I have full physical, legal, and sole custody of D'sani and an order of protection is being put into place as we speak. Don't try to find us."

The anger that appeared in Dominic's face didn't scare me. I took the steps that I needed to escape. I was going to be free. D'sani and Keana stood at the doorway smiling, waiting on me. This was my new life, and nothing was going to hold me back from getting it.

"You stupid bitch!" I heard Dominic bark. Instinctively, I turned around and Dominic's face was twisted up.

Click! Click! Boom!

The whole place was silent. One alligator, two alligator, three alligator; three seconds was all it took for it to register in someone's head that a gun was involved. Pandemonium erupted, but I was frozen in place. My beautiful white dress was painted red now from the bullet wound nestled in my stomach. Dominic came close to me with a sick smile on his face. He raised his arm, the barrel of the gun in my face.

"If I can't have you, nobody can."

Don't you stop loving me
Don't you quit loving me
Just start loving me…
Must be love on the brain

Gasping, I sat up in bed and pressed my hand against my stomach. My hands shook as I tried to hold them steady to see if they came back bloody. Relief washed over me as I realized that every single thing that had just happened was just a dream. My body was covered in sweat and D'sani was lying right next to me, undisturbed. My mind was foggy because that dream felt like real life, from Dominic giving me the sweetest love all the way up to the wedding. I looked at the time on the clock next to the bed and it read that it was seven o' clock at night. Thank God it was the weekend because I knew D'sani was going to be up all night.

"D'sani, come on, get up," I said, shaking her awake.

I grabbed my phone and went downstairs to throw a frozen pizza in the oven. The couch became our best friend as I tried to contact Dominic. His phone went straight to voicemail. I called about four times before I heard him trying to get inside the house door. Just as I began to open the door, he came in. My eyes bugged, and my mouth dropped. He was wearing the same thing he had on in my dream and smelled of alcohol.

"What the fuck are you looking at? Go get me a damn beer," he slurred as he stepped into the living room, taking his shoes off.

Grabbing D'sani by the hand, I rushed to the kitchen and grabbed Dominic a beer. In my mind I repeated the word "no" several times. My dream wasn't about to become a reality. Dominic didn't notice me slip inside the kitchen to grab my phone, nor did he notice that I had slipped shoes on and D'sani and I were headed out of the house.

I got to the end of the driveway, holding my breath, and immediately exhaled when I saw a dark-colored truck coming in our direction. I prayed that they saw me flailing my arms and had the heart to stop. I jumped with joy when they did. The window crept down, and I couldn't be happier to see who was behind the wheel.

"Why are you in the middle of the street? You need some help?" Nolan asked with a concerned look on his face.

"Yes, please," I practically begged, looking behind me to make sure that Dominic was still in the house.

"Well, get in."

I opened the back door and placed D'sani inside and made sure that she was buckled in tight with the seatbelt. Next, I ran over to the passenger side and got ready to climb in. Dominic opened the door and drunkenly began to scream my name. Nolan looked at me and I returned a look that begged him to press down the gas and go.

"Please. I will explain later. I just need to get away as far as I can and now."

Dominic was moving closer to the car and was screaming obscenities, acting like a crazy person. Nolan put his car in drive and sped away. My heart didn't relax until we were ten minutes away and on the highway, leaving Schenectady to head to Albany. The ride was silent as he made his way through the Albany streets, ending up on Sherman Street. He turned the car off and sat back in his seat. My throat was dry, and I didn't even know where I should begin.

"Thank you for do this for me and my daughter," I managed to say, my voice hoarse and mannish.

"Mah'lani, what the fuck just happened?" he asked. He realized that D'sani was in the car and excused his language.

"I will explain. I just need to get her something to eat."

Without another word, Nolan took me to McDonald's to get D'sani some food. He had to pay because my dumb ass forgot to grab some money. My main concern was getting out of there and making sure my dream didn't manifest. We arrived back on Sherman Street as he helped me out of the car and assisted me up the stairs while I held D'sani in my arms. Inside of the two-story house, he showed me to the dining room table, where I helped D'sani take a seat and placed her food in front of her. Nolan stood off to the side and watched me attentively until I made my way over to him.

"You gonna tell me now?" Nolan asked.

"If you have the time to listen."

"I don't have nowhere to be. In case you didn't notice, I just picked up the woman that I have been crushing on and her child, running from a maniac drunk."

As bad as I wanted to laugh at his joke, I couldn't. It was hard for me to register that I was away from Dominic and in another man's presence, someone that wasn't Malcolm or Randy. I took a seat on the couch and told him to prepare himself for a long story.

I told him everything. Things that not even Keana knew. This was my last chance at reaching out and I was going to make it count. Along the story there were tears, ugly crying, and hiccups, but Nolan was there, listening to me release my burdens, and only spoke when he had a question to better understand something that I told him.

Nolan told me that I could stay if I needed and he would give me the bedroom that he had downstairs to me and D'sani.

He also suggested that I call Keana and tell her what was going on and to not tell Randy where I was. I needed her to grab me and D'sani some clothes and money and like a best friend, she was there. She was there within an hour and a half with new clothes for us and she gave me fifteen hundred dollars. She told me if I needed more that she wouldn't mind giving it to me until I was able to access my bank cards. She also bought a new phone, already activated, and threw my old one away. She said that I needed to be rid of Dominic altogether. She thanked Nolan before leaving. I followed up with my own thanks yet again and a hug. I was truly grateful for him and for that, I was forever in debt to him, whether he liked it or not.

Mimi

Epilogue

Two months later
No time for moping around, are you kidding?
And no time for negative vibes, cause I'm winning
It's been a long week, I put in my hardest
Gonna live my life, feels so good to get it right

A woman who changes her hair is about to change her life, said Coco Chanel. I couldn't have agreed more with that statement. My hair was now in a pixie cut, dyed a light burgundy. I had been Dominic-free for two months and had been the happiest at this time. Even though I hadn't seen him, it didn't mean that I trusted him to stay away. There was an order of protection in place and if I knew Dominic, I knew that he was not gonna let a piece of paper stand in his way. Clarissa had drawn up an emergency order like I knew she would and presented it to me. Only my name was on it and to be honest, I preferred it that way.

The first two weeks of me going back to work, Keana and Clarissa argued with me that I needed more time off. I wholeheartedly thought I was great and wanted to get back to work. We went back and forth for a week until I threatened to get transferred to a different office. After that, there was nothing else from Clarissa, but Keana, not so much. Every chance she got, she was down my neck.

It was a Friday night, Clarissa offered to babysit D'sani for me while I went to go have fun with Keana. This was the first time that D'sani was going to be out of my sight besides school, and I was a bit worried.

"Go and have fun. You have nothing to worry about. No one knows where I live except family. If somebody even thought about coming up on my porch, they would meet the tip of my fo'fo," she assured me, causing me to laugh.

I relaxed just a tad bit and gave D'sani kisses before I left to meet Keana. Our adventure took us out to Troy. We were going to The Bradley, a small bar on Fourth Street that had karaoke.

"How do you feel about being away from D'sani?" Nolan asked.

"You just had to go and ask, right? I was good, but now she's gonna be on my mind." I crossed my arms and pouted.

Nolan laughed and responded, "Girl, cut that out and poke your lip in. Let's get in there and have some fun. But just so you know, she's on my mind too. She's only been around me for a short period, but that little girl won my heart."

"I guess. Come on. Keana probably having a heart attack waiting on us."

We exited the car and walked into the bar. I spotted Keana right away sitting at the bar and nursing a drink. Randy was sitting next to her, and I wasn't ready for this. Although I knew him, I was pretty sure that he would have run back and told Dominic he had seen me and that I was with a dude. Nolan and I were strictly friends, but let Dominic find that out and he would be on a manhunt looking for both myself and Nolan. I hesitated before I walked over, and that was enough time for Keana to realize that I had been standing there, and she waved us over.

"Hey, girl. What's up, Randy?" I stated with a little salt in my voice.

Randy turned in his stool and took one look at me and turned giddy like a child. "Hey, sis! It's fucking good to see you, and you look good too," he said, giving me a hug. Keana sat off to the side with a smile as wide as the Mississippi River on her face.

She interrupted and said, "I told you she did. She got her glow back and homegirl gained back some happy weight and it looks good." She peered on the side of me and noticed Nolan, and I knew she was gonna say something smart. She continued, speaking to Nolan, "What's up, punk ass?"

"Shut ya ole ugly ass up," Nolan spit back. They stared each other down and before Randy could take them seriously, they both burst into laughter.

"Randy, this is Nolan. Nolan, this is Randy. Keana's boyfriend." I took the liberty of introducing them and like men do, they gave each other a pound.

"What y'all drinking on?" Randy asked.

"Oh, nothing but water for me. It's all about Mah'lani tonight. I'm driving."

"Well, in that case, I'll take two shots of Patron with lime and a tequila and orange juice."

"You got it," Randy stated and turned to order our drinks.

When they came, Nolan and Randy slid off to go play darts while Keana and I sat at the bar talking and drinking. Before I knew it, my face was hot, and I was a tad bit tipsy.

"Look at you, so happy," Keana stated.

"It's been a long time coming. I was dragged through the dirt, even in my dreams, but here I am still standing."

"And that's how it should be. I'm happy that you're happy. You know who else I'm happy for? Quinn. She had her baby not too long ago. Both of you women deserve the world for the shit that you both went through."

"What did she have? When you speak with her, let her know I said congratulations."

"A girl. It's something in the air because everybody having little girls."

"Aww. Speaking of, I should call to check to see if D'sani is okay."

"No. She's fine. If Clarissa hasn't called you, there ain't nothing wrong," Keana said.

I believed her. It was just the protective nature that I had in me.

"Has anyone seen him?" I asked. I shouldn't be asking, but I needed to know.

Keana looked at me with a why-you-asking-about-him look. I should have known that I was going to get that look. For my assurance, I needed to know.

She sighed and said, "No. No one has seen him. Not even Randy. He's been going by the house to see if he's there, but every time he goes, his car is missing, and he has a growing pile of mail. Nothing with your name on it. Even though you lived there. That trifling bastard probably clocking just your mail to see if he could track you down. The cops better catch him before I do because if I see him today or ten years from now, he goes in the dirt."

"Listen to you, gangsta."

"Nah, real talk. But let's get up and dance and get off this sappy shit. We came out to have fun and guess what? That's what we gonna do."

"I agree with that."

Keana was the first to get up. She made her way to the jukebox and paid for a whole album of ninety's reggae to be played. She knew just what I liked and what to get me moving. "Boom Bye Bye" by Buju Banton came on first and I slid to the dance floor, winding my hips, catching the attention of Nolan. He stopped throwing the darts and watched me closely. A smile appeared on my face and my face grew hot from his hypnotizing stare. He moved in my direction, stalking, like a tiger on its prey. One he was in my bubble, he stood behind me, my butt on his manhood, and he matched my moves. Our bodies moved together like they belonged together. We caught the attention of all the partygoers as we did everything but take our clothes off to fuck. Keana, being her normal self, was hyping it up in the background while Randy watched the crowd and our surroundings.

Buju Banton quickly switched to Lil Vicious's "Freak", hyping everybody. Every woman inside the bar was on the dance floor, taking part in an ass shaking contest that none of us had any business partaking in. We couldn't help it. Positive vibes were in the air and I was feeling great.

Three songs later I needed to take a break, use the bathroom, and drink some water. I dragged Keana by the arm as we went to the bathroom together. We talked about all the little booty chicks who was trying to keep up with the big booty ones. We laughed so hard we were damn near on the floor, cracking up and holding our stomachs. Five minutes later, our laughs ceased, and we walked out of the bathroom.

Upon exiting the bathroom, something told me to look towards the bar, and when I did I almost pissed myself, even though I had just relieved myself. His back was turned but his face was facing the mirrors behind the bar and he was looking right at me. I felt my face draining of all color as he looked back at me with his cold eyes. *Nah, that's a ghost. It can't be Dominic,* I told myself. I clamped my eyelids shut and waited a few seconds before I opened them. Looking in the direction where I thought he had been sitting, I saw that there was no one there occupying the seat. My heartbeat tried slowing, but I felt someone behind me. I turned around and was prepared to swing, but realized that it was Nolan.

"Aye! You cool? It's me," he said, throwing his hands up.

"Yeah, I'm okay. Sorry," I said managing a smile.

"You sure? You look like you saw a ghost."

"Yes, I'm sure. What's up? You ready to go?" I asked. I knew I was after I done spooked myself.

"No. I was just coming to let you know that I was going to step out to smoke a cigarette. I didn't want you to be looking for me thinking I went missing or something."

"Oh, okay. Thank you. Don't take too long. I'm ready to finish dancing," I flirted.

"Word?" Nolan asked, making the face that Carmelo Anthony does in the meme on Facebook. I threw my head back and laughed.

"Yes. Go ahead and go smoke. I'm gonna just get some water and sober up some. I am feeling a little hot."

"Good. I'll be back."

Our eyes lingered a bit on each other. He was the first to break the stare.

I walked over to the bar and asked for a bottled water, looking into the crowd. I watched as Keana and Randy mashed their bodies together and danced to "Romantic Call" by Patra. Life had really changed for the better for the both of us and I was satisfied with us being happy. I never thought that she was going to take anyone serious and here she was, in a relationship, being happy. Me, I wasn't where I wanted to be, but I was healing daily to regain my strength physically and mentally. Nolan had been my blessing in disguise. He didn't have to take D'sani and me in, but he did. He came running when I would wake up screaming from the nightmares that I would have and would stay up late with me, making sure that I was okay to go back to sleep.

I was nowhere near being ready to climb into a relationship just yet, but I had a feeling when I was ready, Nolan would be there waiting for me. He was good with D'sani and she adored him. From time to time she would call for her daddy and all I could do was tell her that he was away on vacation and would be back soon. It broke my heart that it had to be that way, but I had to do it to protect her. Yeah, yeah,

170

yeah, she's his child, but he didn't want her. He only dealt with her because I had kept her around. He had no choice but to be nice and interact. She officially belonged to me and I would protect her until my last breath.

Keana saw me sitting at the bar by myself and made her way over to me. Sweat was on her forehead and a smile on her face. She said, "Girl, why you not on the dance floor?"

"I was talking to Nolan, but he went to go smoke a cigarette. I thought I saw Dominic sitting at the bar and almost died right here. I need to sober up some."

"You want me to have Randy check around just to make sure?"

"No, y'all having fun. I don't think he's here. I was probably just seeing shit!"

The bar erupted in chaos and people damn near trampled each other to find an exit. Randy was next to us in seconds, grabbing us by the arms to led us to safety. Women were screaming, wigs and fake Timbs were flying all over the place, and finally the music cut off. The sirens could be heard in the distance and I knew something tragic happened.

"Wait, Randy! Nolan! He went out to go smoke!" I yelled.

"I'm pretty sure he good, sis. We need to get out of here safely!"

I wanted to listen, but my gut was eating me up and telling me to go out the front. The last time I ignored my gut, I got my ass beaten as if it was a sport. I twisted away from Randy and made my way through the crowd. Elbows, hands, fingers, and possibly a foot touched me as I tried to get out.

The cool night air welcomed me as I made it through the door. There were people standing around and I decided to go up to ask a female what happened.

"Somebody was shooting," she said with a somber tone.

"Where?" I asked.

She pointed in the direction of where Nolan had parked the car.

Keana and Randy met me in the front and asked me what happened. My heart pounded in my chest. I heard Keana calling my name, but it was like I was hearing her underwater. She was holding onto my arm, but I ran away from her towards the direction where Nolan had parked the car. Police were arriving there just as I was and already putting up the yellow tape. There was a female officer on the scene and she caught me in her arms as I tried to get past. Nolan's car was riddled with bullet holes. I wasn't sure if there was a body. The female officer kept telling me to calm down and I couldn't, wouldn't listen.

"Mah'lani, you have to relax. We don't know if it's him or not," Keana said, trying to calm me down.

My chest was tight. My bones told me what I didn't need to know.

"There's no pulse!" I heard a policeman yell.

"Noooooo!" I yelled.

"Ma'am, do you know what happened here?" the female cop asked.

"No! I came in that car and I need to check and see if it's my friend."

The female cop looked at me. She walked over to another cop and spoke to him. He nodded his head and told me to follow her. Keana wasn't too far behind holding my head. The air was cold and whipping around me like it wanted to kick my ass. The officer led me over to a body covered with a white sheet. Keana held me tight as they held me close. His face had a bullet hole in it, but I knew it was him by his shirt.

"Nooooooo. Nolannnnn! My God! Nolan!" I yelled as I collapsed into Keana's arms. There was no calming me now.

The wind whipped and just as sure as I was in my dream about hearing that word "leave", in my reality I heard, "I told you, if I can't have you, nobody can."

But what made it real for me was the footsteps that walked away.

The End

Submission Guideline

Submit the first three chapters of your completed manuscript to ldpsubmissions@gmail.com, subject line: Your book's title. The manuscript must be in a .doc file and sent as an attachment. Document should be in Times New Roman, double spaced and in size 12 font. Also, provide your synopsis and full contact information. If sending multiple submissions, they must each be in a separate email.

Have a story but no way to send it electronically? You can still submit to LDP/Ca$h Presents. Send in the first three chapters, written or typed, of your completed manuscript to:

LDP: Submissions Dept
Po Box 870494
Mesquite, Tx 75187

DO NOT send original manuscript. Must be a duplicate.

Provide your synopsis and a cover letter containing your full contact information.

Thanks for considering LDP and Ca$h Presents.

Crime of Passion 2

BOW DOWN TO MY GANGSTA

By **Ca$h**

TORN BETWEEN TWO

By **Coffee**

BLOOD STAINS OF A SHOTTA **III**

By **Jamaica**

STEADY MOBBIN **III**

By **Marcellus Allen**

BLOOD OF A BOSS **V**

By **Askari**

LOYAL TO THE GAME **IV**

LIFE OF SIN II

By **T.J. & Jelissa**

A DOPEBOY'S PRAYER **II**

By **Eddie "Wolf" Lee**

IF LOVING YOU IS WRONG... **III**

LOVE ME EVEN WHEN IT HURTS **II**

By **Jelissa**

TRUE SAVAGE **VI**

By **Chris Green**

BLAST FOR ME **III**

A BRONX TALE

DUFFLE BAG CARTEL

By **Ghost**

ADDICTIED TO THE DRAMA **III**

Mimi

By **Jamila Mathis**
LIPSTICK KILLAH **III**
WHAT BAD BITCHES DO **III**
KILL ZONE **II**
By **Aryanna**
THE COST OF LOYALTY **II**
By **Kweli**
SHE FELL IN LOVE WITH A REAL ONE **II**
By **Tamara Butler**
LOVE SHOULDN'T HURT **III**
RENEGADE BOYS **III**
By **Meesha**
CORRUPTED BY A GANGSTA **IV**
By **Destiny Skai**
A GANGSTER'S CODE **III**
By **J-Blunt**
KING OF NEW YORK III
By **T.J. Edwards**
GORILLAS IN THE BAY II
De'Kari
THE STREETS ARE CALLING II
Duquie Wilson
KINGPIN KILLAZ III
Hood Rich
STEADY MOBBIN' **III**
Marcellus Allen
SINS OF A HUSTLA II

ASAD

HER MAN, MINE'S TOO **II**

CASH MONEY HOES

Nicole Goosby

TRIGGADALE II

Elijah R. Freeman

<u>**Available Now**</u>

<u>RESTRAINING ORDER **I & II**</u>

By **CA$H & Coffee**

<u>LOVE KNOWS NO BOUNDARIES **I II & III**</u>

By **Coffee**

<u>RAISED AS A GOON I, II, III & IV</u>

<u>BRED BY THE SLUMS I, II, III</u>

<u>BLAST FOR ME I & II</u>

<u>ROTTEN TO THE CORE I III</u>

By **Ghost**

<u>LAY IT DOWN **I & II**</u>

<u>LAST OF A DYING BREED</u>

<u>BLOOD STAINS OF A SHOTTA I & II</u>

By **Jamaica**

<u>LOYAL TO THE GAME</u>

<u>LOYAL TO THE GAME II</u>

<u>LOYAL TO THE GAME III</u>

<u>LIFE OF SIN</u>

By **TJ & Jelissa**

BLOODY COMMAS I & II

SKI MASK CARTEL I II & III

KING OF NEW YORK I II

By **T.J. Edwards**

IF LOVING HIM IS WRONG…I & II

LOVE ME EVEN WHEN IT HURTS

By **Jelissa**

WHEN THE STREETS CLAP BACK I & II III

By **Jibril Williams**

A DISTINGUISHED THUG STOLE MY HEART I II & III

LOVE SHOULDN'T HURT I II

RENEGADE BOYS I & II

By **Meesha**

A GANGSTER'S CODE I & II

By **J-Blunt**

PUSH IT TO THE LIMIT

By **Bre' Hayes**

BLOOD OF A BOSS **I, II, III & IV**

By **Askari**

THE STREETS BLEED MURDER **I, II & III**

THE HEART OF A GANGSTA I II& III

By **Jerry Jackson**

CUM FOR ME

CUM FOR ME 2

CUM FOR ME 3

CUM FOR ME 4

An **LDP Erotica Collaboration**

BRIDE OF A HUSTLA **I II & II**

THE FETTI GIRLS **I, II& III**

CORRUPTED BY A GANGSTA I, II & III

By **Destiny Skai**

WHEN A GOOD GIRL GOES BAD

By **Adrienne**

A GANGSTER'S REVENGE **I II III & IV**

THE BOSS MAN'S DAUGHTERS

THE BOSS MAN'S DAUGHTERS II

THE BOSSMAN'S DAUGHTERS III

THE BOSSMAN'S DAUGHTERS IV

THE BOSS MAN'S DAUGHTERS **V**

A SAVAGE LOVE **I & II**

BAE BELONGS TO ME

A HUSTLER'S DECEIT I, II

WHAT BAD BITCHES DO I, II

By **Aryanna**

A KINGPIN'S AMBITON

A KINGPIN'S AMBITION **II**

I MURDER FOR THE DOUGH

By **Ambitious**

TRUE SAVAGE

TRUE SAVAGE II

TRUE SAVAGE **III**

TRUE SAVAGE **IV**

TRUE SAVAGE **V**

By **Chris Green**

Mimi

A DOPEBOY'S PRAYER
By **Eddie "Wolf" Lee**
THE KING CARTEL **I, II & III**
By **Frank Gresham**
THESE NIGGAS AIN'T LOYAL **I, II & III**
By **Nikki Tee**
GANGSTA SHYT **I II &III**
By **CATO**
THE ULTIMATE BETRAYAL
By **Phoenix**
BOSS'N UP **I , II & III**
By **Royal Nicole**
I LOVE YOU TO DEATH
By Destiny J
I RIDE FOR MY HITTA
I STILL RIDE FOR MY HITTA
By **Misty Holt**
LOVE & CHASIN' PAPER
By **Qay Crockett**
TO DIE IN VAIN
SINS OF A HUSTLA
By **ASAD**
BROOKLYN HUSTLAZ
By **Boogsy Morina**
BROOKLYN ON LOCK I & II
By **Sonovia**
GANGSTA CITY

180

By **Teddy Duke**

<u>A DRUG KING AND HIS DIAMOND I & II III</u>

<u>A DOPEMAN'S RICHES</u>

<u>HER MAN, MINE'S TOO</u>

By Nicole Goosby

<u>TRAPHOUSE KING **I II & III**</u>

<u>KINGPIN KILLAZ</u>

By **Hood Rich**

<u>LIPSTICK KILLAH **I, II**</u>

<u>CRIME OF PASSION I & II</u>

By **Mimi**

<u>STEADY MOBBN' **I, II**</u>

By **Marcellus Allen**

<u>WHO SHOT YA **I, II**</u>

Renta

<u>GORILLAZ IN THE BAY</u>

DE'KARI

<u>TRIGGADALE</u>

Elijah R. Freeman

<u>GOD BLESS THE TRAPPERS I, II, III</u>

<u>THESE SCANDALOUS STREETS I, II, III</u>

<u>FEAR MY GANGSTA I, II, III</u>

<u>THESE STREETS DON'T LOVE NOBODY I, II</u>

Tranay Adams

<u>THE STREETS ARE CALLING</u>

Duquie Wilson

Mimi

BOOKS BY LDP'S CEO, CA$H

TRUST IN NO MAN

TRUST IN NO MAN 2

TRUST IN NO MAN 3

BONDED BY BLOOD

SHORTY GOT A THUG

THUGS CRY

THUGS CRY 2

THUGS CRY 3

TRUST NO BITCH

TRUST NO BITCH 2

TRUST NO BITCH 3

TIL MY CASKET DROPS

RESTRAINING ORDER

RESTRAINING ORDER 2

IN LOVE WITH A CONVICT

Coming Soon

BONDED BY BLOOD 2

BOW DOWN TO MY GANGSTA

Mimi